HOMICIDE IN BERLIN

David Brunelle Legal Thriller #12

STEPHEN PENNER

ISBN 13: 9780578697321

Homicide in Berlin

Joy Lorton, Editor.
Cover design by Nathan Wampler Book Covers.

THE DAVID BRUNELLE LEGAL THRILLERS

HOMICIDE
IN BERLIN

Injustice anywhere is a threat to justice everywhere.

~Dr. Martin Luther King, Jr.

CHAPTER 1

"You wouldn't catch me dead in there."

David Brunelle, homicide prosecutor and European traveler, gazed down at the hole in the tiled spa floor. It was three feet square, ten feet deep, and filled to the brim with ice cold water. The metal handrail with steps leading into the water confirmed it wasn't an architectural mistake or decorative water feature. The spa owners actually expected people to drop themselves vertically into its frozen depths.

"I don't know..." Casey Emory, police detective and American girlfriend, peered at the post-sauna 'cold plunge' pool. "Looks invigorating."

"More like de-vigorating," Brunelle returned. "That would stop my heart."

"So, I *would* catch you dead in there," Casey laughed, "if you went in."

"Which I won't," Brunelle answered. "So, no, you wouldn't."

They were at Spa Balibai, the latest and greatest luxury spa in Berlin, hidden away in a residential neighborhood in the northwest of Germany's capital city. Brunelle had taken a leave of absence from his job at the King County Prosecuting Attorney's Office in Seattle, USA. Casey had taken the opportunity to cash in some of her accrued vacation and book them a two-week trip to Europe. Actually, the entire two weeks was in Berlin.

Brunelle had never been to Germany. Casey was stationed there for two years before becoming a cop and had been wanting to come back and brush up on her German ever since. Those two years had been on an Air Force base outside of Frankfurt. The spa in Berlin was undeniably more luxurious.

Brunelle was loving it too.

"Come on." He tugged Casey away from the Ice Pool of Death and toward the large monitor screen on the wall. He started tapping at the glass. "Let's schedule another couple's massage. We've got just enough time before the restaurant opens for dinner."

"And drinks," Casey added.

"And drinks," Brunelle agreed as he confirmed their reservation in the massage wing of the sprawling complex. "There, we're booked. Starts in five minutes. Let's go."

* * *

"Let's stay," Brunelle groaned several hours later. He ran a hand over his short-cropped, graying hair, still slightly damp from one last dip in the heated outdoor pool, lit from below against the dark German evening. After dinner, drinks, and yet another couple's massage, it was finally closing time at Spa Balibai. "There's like a million waterbed lounge chairs here," Brunelle continued, "and they're heated! I bet they wouldn't even notice if we curled up on a couple of those in some back corner."

"I bet they would," Casey laughed. She had skipped the

last dip in the pool, her soft black curls dangling unkempt and natural on her brown shoulders. "And I don't think they'd find it amusing. The Germans aren't known for their sense of humor."

Brunelle thought for a moment, then nodded vaguely at the spa surrounding them. "It's a Hawaiian theme, not German. I think we're good."

"It's Indonesian, Mr. Culturally Sensitive." Casey shook her head at him. "And if we stay after closing, it's trespassing. The last thing I want to do is commit a crime in a foreign country. Even Germany."

"Especially Germany," Brunelle said. "I don't even speak German."

"*Gefängnis*," Casey said as she stood up and slapped Brunelle's leg for him to follow her.

"What does that mean?" he asked, without making any effort whatsoever to stand up.

"Jail," Casey translated. "Now come on. Let's change back into our street clothes. We can come back tomorrow if you want."

"Oh yeah, Davey want," Brunelle replied, finally standing up.

Casey cocked her head then shook it at him. "How drunk are you?"

"How do you say 'very' in German?" Brunelle asked.

"*Sehr*," Casey answered.

"Yeah, not quite that." Brunelle pointed at her. "But close. One more drink?"

"Goodbye, 'Davey'," she called out over her shoulder as she turned toward the locker rooms. "I'll see you in the lobby in ten minutes, or in the *Gefängnis* in ten hours. Your choice."

"Ten hours?" Brunelle gasped. "You wouldn't bail me out right away?"

"I don't even know if they have bail here." She turned around and put a fist on her hip. "And anyway, I didn't come here to get involved in more crime. I came to get away from it. Don't ruin that for me."

Brunelle sighed. "Fine." He trudged forward. "You're probably right. This place is so nice, trespassing is probably the worst crime anyone would ever dare commit here."

"Then let's not be those people," Casey concluded. "Let's be the people who change clothes and leave right at closing and maybe come back again and don't trespass."

Brunelle finally gave in. "Okay." He quickened his gait toward the changing rooms. "But no 'maybe'. We are definitely coming back here again."

The spa was clothes-optional—"Europe," Brunelle had scoffed—but most patrons wore the long white robes provided by the spa. Just not all of the robes were cinched closed. In any event, it should have been a quick matter to drop the robe in the designated hamper and change back into the clothes Brunelle had worn there, but he was a little more buzzed than he realized, so his movements were slow as he reluctantly pulled the real world back onto his body. His clothes felt strange on his skin after a full day of saunas and massages, so it wasn't until he stepped into the lobby where Casey was already waiting that he noticed his back pocket didn't have his wallet in it.

"Oh, crap," he said patting at his pockets.

"What's wrong?" Casey asked. She couldn't help stealing a glance at the clock. They were already several minutes past closing.

"My wallet's missing," Brunelle explained.

"You left your wallet at the hotel," Casey reminded him, "so it wouldn't be stolen. Remember? You only brought that one credit card so we could pay admission and buy drinks."

"Oh, yeah." Another self-pat-down. "Well then, that one credit card is missing. I must have left it at the bar by the outdoor pool."

Casey rolled her eyes and made no effort to suppress an exasperated sigh. "Is this some trick so we get locked in tonight? It's already after closing. We're already trespassing."

"It's not trespassing," Brunelle countered. "We have a necessity defense."

"Do you even know if they have necessity as a defense here?" Casey challenged.

"Do you even know if they have trespassing as a crime here?" Brunelle rejoined. "Come on. Let's just run back to the bar and ask if they have it."

"You can't ask that," Casey pointed out. "You don't speak German."

"I know." Brunelle nodded at her. "That's why I said, 'let's run back to the bar', and not, 'you wait here while I run back to the bar'."

Casey sighed again. "I swear to God. If you get me arrested…"

"I promise," Brunelle grabbed her hand and pulled her back toward the interior of the spa, "you will not interact with the local law enforcement authorities tonight."

Casey shook her head at him but let herself get pulled back into the spa.

The quickest way to the bar was through the entry foyer, past the small indoor pool, out the door by the saunas, past the cold plunge pool, and around to the other side of the large outdoor pool. The blue lights that had lit the outside pools were already turned off, so it was very dark outside. Brunelle almost didn't notice the one other patron who had also apparently decided to stay after hours, for one last quick plunge in the Ice Pool of Death.

What Brunelle did notice, after his initial surprise, was that the man's plunge wasn't quick at all. In fact, the man was just floating in the water, only the very top of his head above the waterline.

Brunelle stopped in his tracks, pulling Casey back to him.

"What now?" she demanded. "We need to get out of here."

Brunelle pointed at the cold plunge pool. Casey's gaze followed his finger to see the body bobbing in the water. They both waited a few more moments to confirm the person wasn't simply holding his breath. He wasn't.

"I guess I lied," Brunelle finally said. "We are definitely interacting with the local law enforcement authorities tonight."

CHAPTER 2

The local law enforcement authority who spoke with them was younger than Brunelle had expected. Or rather, it was the combination of apparent youth and apparent rank that surprised Brunelle. He was in plain clothes, like a detective, but looked barely thirty. Maybe it was his hairstyle, black hair combed forward from the crown like a little boy, but with specks of salt in the mostly pepper. Maybe it was his face, still chubby with baby fat, but with the beginnings of wrinkles at his eyes. Or maybe Brunelle was just terrible at guessing people's ages.

"*Guten Abend. Ich bin Kommissaranwärter Dieter Vorsburg,*" the local law enforcement authority said as he approached Brunelle and Casey. They were sitting on the brick wall of a large planter just inside the doors that led out to the Ice Pool of Actual Death. "*Ich möchte Ihnen ein paar Fragen stellen.*"

Brunelle blinked at the unintelligible words the man had thrown at them. Casey had taught him one German phrase to use in case they got separated. So, he decided to try it out for the first time.

"Um, my *Frau* can *Deutsch,*" Brunelle staggered, "uh, but

ich nicht."

Casey smiled at her boyfriend's effort then looked up at the policeman. "He doesn't speak German," she explained in English.

"Yes," the policeman replied, also in English. "I can see that."

He took out a cigarette and lit it, even though they were inside. After a long first drag, he tried again, in perfect, if slightly accented English. "Good evening. I am Junior Inspector Dieter Vorsburg. I would like to ask you a few questions."

Brunelle relaxed visibly. "Oh, good," he exhaled. "There was no way I was going to be able to do this in German."

"Obviously," Vorsburg agreed. "You are Americans?"

"Yes," Casey answered for them. "We're here on holiday."

"Americans say 'vacation', yes?" Vorsburg half-corrected her. "I studied for a year in the U.S.A. while I was at university."

"In college," Casey teased. "We say 'in college'."

"Yes, I remember that now." Vorsburg smiled. "I very much liked America. You have such the entrepreneurial spirit, yes? Everything can be done by the private sector. Some places even have private police forces, isn't that right?"

"I do not think that is right," Casey answered. "I very much hope that is not right."

"Um, not to interrupt," Brunelle interrupted, "but are we gonna talk about the dead guy in the pool? I mean, I really don't mind spending all night here, but I would have preferred a quiet night on a waterbed lounge chair."

"Uh, yes, certainly," Vorsburg replied. Then he took a moment to appraise the two Americans. "Neither of you seem particularly upset at having found a dead body. Permit me to say that I find that curious."

"Suspicious," Casey said. "You mean you find it suspicious."

Vorsburg offered another grin. "Perhaps I do," he agreed. "Would I be right to be suspicious, Miss...?"

"Ms.," Casey corrected. "Ms. Casey Emory. *Detective* Casey Emory, in fact."

Vorsburg's eyes lit up. "Detective? You are a police officer?"

Casey nodded. "I am."

"And you?" Vorsburg asked Brunelle, his voice animated. "Are you a police officer also?"

"No, he's just a prosecutor," Casey answered for her boyfriend.

Brunelle scowled at her. "A *homicide* prosecutor," he elaborated. "I've stood over my share of dead bodies, Inspector Vorsburg. Just never one bobbing in a pool like a Halloween apple."

"Halloween apple?" Casey questioned. "What's that?"

"You bob for apples at Halloween," Brunelle explained. "Halloween apple."

"No one says that," Casey shook her head at him.

"Maybe they do when they're on holiday at university," Brunelle suggested with a sneer.

Casey rolled her eyes and looked at the policeman. "I'm sorry, Inspector Vorsburg—"

Dieter's coy grin had melted into a genuinely warm smile. "Oh, no, no, no," he interrupted. "You don't have to call me Inspector Vorsburg. We are colleagues, you and I. Call me Dieter. May I call you Casey?"

"Of course," Casey replied. She gestured to Brunelle.

"And this is Davey."

Brunelle dropped his shoulders and looked crossways at his girlfriend. "Really?"

"Casey and Davey," Dieter repeated, visibly excited. "Wonderful. Wonderful. It is truly a pleasure to meet you. I really enjoyed your country when I lived there 'in college'. It is a pleasure to host you now in my country."

"Host?" Brunelle questioned. "Don't you mean interrogate?"

Dieter laughed. "Oh, I don't need to interrogate you. You found the man, but you didn't kill him." A pause, then another playful grin. "Or perhaps you did?"

"We did *not* kill him," Brunelle confirmed. He wasn't looking for trouble. For all he knew, this was some form of German interrogation technique. "Do you want us to make a statement or something? Explain how we found the body? Our initial observations? Who we contacted and how long it took to do so?"

Dieter chuckled and waved away the suggestion, lit cigarette between his fingers. "Oh no, not now. It is very late. I only wanted to see if you were all right. Most people would be upset at finding a dead body floating like a Halloween apple."

"Bobbing," Brunelle corrected.

"No one says that!" Casey repeated, exasperated.

"But now I see you are very all right," Dieter continued. "Why don't you come to the police station tomorrow morning, and you can make your statement then? Go back to your hotel for now. Get some rest. Then, after you've made your statements, I can give you a tour, show you how we do things here in Berlin. How does that sound?"

Casey looked at Brunelle, and they both nodded in

agreement.

"That sounds great," Casey answered for them.

"So, we definitely have to go back to our hotel?" Brunelle lamented.

Casey smacked him. But Dieter seemed to think he was serious. "You would rather spend the night at the scene of a murder?"

"I've spent plenty of nights at murder scenes," Brunelle answered. "But I've never spent the night on a heated waterbed lounge chair."

CHAPTER 3

Junior Inspector Dieter Vorsburg worked out of the Berlin Police Headquarters building on the city's Platz der Luftbrücke plaza, in what had been the American sector of town when Berlin was still divided east and west. *Luftbrücke* meant 'air bridge', and was named in honor of the Berlin Airlift, complete with a memorial statue meant to suggest planes taking off toward what used to be West Germany. The plaza was only a short subway ride from the hotel where Brunelle and Casey did, in fact, spend the night.

"This should be interesting," Brunelle commented as they reached the top of the stairs from the subway, or '*U-Bahn*', station.

"It's already interesting," Casey replied. "Why wouldn't they just take our statements last night? Why make us come back? I mean, what if we didn't come back? That detective didn't even ask what hotel we were staying at. How would they find us?"

"The spa has my credit card number," Brunelle answered. "It's only like two steps to get a list of our other purchases. Then just look for a hotel charge in Berlin."

Casey shrugged. "Yeah, I guess you're right."

"Of course, I am," Brunelle laughed. "I'm Davey Brunelle."

Casey laughed too. "I dare you to keep that up."

But Brunelle shook his head. "Oh, no. The first thing I'm going to do is correct that little mistake."

"That hilarious mistake," Casey countered.

"Whatever." Brunelle pulled open the door to the police station lobby. "That detective didn't seem particularly interested in us, let alone the case. He probably doesn't even remember our names."

"Davey! Casey!" Dieter called out as soon as they stepped into the front lobby. He tapped his watch. "And you are right on time as well. That is an excellent habit. Welcome to the headquarters of the Berlin Police."

"So much for that," Brunelle whispered.

But before Brunelle could correct Dieter about his name, Casey jumped in. "*Kommissar* Vorsburg. Dieter." She reached out and shook his hand vigorously. "Thank you for inviting me and Davey to see your headquarters. We're very excited to see how you do things here, especially Davey." She turned back to Brunelle. "Isn't that right, Davey?"

Brunelle hesitated, then sighed. "Yes," he agreed simply. "Super excited."

"Outstanding!" Dieter clapped his hands together. He gestured toward the doors to one side of the receptionists. "Let's start with the Investigations Division. That's where I work."

"What about our statements?" Brunelle whispered to Casey as they followed Dieter toward the doors.

Casey shrugged. "Maybe that's why we're going to Investigations first."

The Investigations Division was down a long hallway decorated with photographs of the city. Judging by the color palette and graininess, Brunelle guessed they were mostly from the 1980s. The handful that appeared brand new, with sharp focus and bright colors, only confirmed his guess as to the rest. When they finally reached their destination, Dieter pulled open the door and announced, "Investigations Division, Berlin Police!"

But Brunelle and Casey didn't go in. The doorway was blocked by a very tall, very stout man with a bushy mustache, bald head, and angry eyes. Or at least irritated eyes.

Dieter noticed their hesitation and finally looked into the office, only to see the man blocking his way as well.

"Vorsburg," the man growled. He followed the name with several more words Brunelle couldn't understand, but it was clear from the man's tone he was not pleased.

Dieter's body language was embarrassed and submissive. It wasn't hard to deduce the large mustached man was his superior in some way. After what was assuredly an apology and an explanation, Dieter switched back to English for the introductions.

"Davey and Casey," he said, "this is my supervisor, *Hauptkommissar* Leptheimer."

"Hello," Casey said to the *Hauptkommissar*.

"Nice to meet you," Brunelle extended a hand.

Leptheimer didn't take it. He just grunted at it then grumbled something at Dieter in German.

Dieter laughed nervously, agreed with a few too many *Ja*'s (Brunelle knew that word), then stepped aside so Leptheimer could exit the office.

After the older, fatter, angrier German policeman had passed, Dieter offered a sheepish grin. "My apologies. Chief

Inspector Leptheimer is not a very friendly man. But he is an excellent police officer. He wanted to know why I had brought two civilians back to our Investigations Division. I had to tell him you were witnesses to the murder last night and had come to the station to make your statements."

"Is that not true?" Brunelle asked. "That is why we're here, right?"

"It's one reason you are here," Dieter admitted. "But truthfully, I wanted to show you our police station. Especially Casey. Police officer to police officer."

"Um, okay," Brunelle replied. "So, are we going to do the tour first or the statements first?"

"I suppose we better do the statements first," Dieter answered. "But that shouldn't take long. It is not as if you actually saw anything important."

"The dead body is probably pretty important," Brunelle whispered to Casey.

"More important is how it got to be dead," Casey replied. "All we can say is that he was dead, not how."

"Probably died from hypothermia," Brunelle joked as they followed Dieter inside.

"Oh, no," Dieter replied over his shoulder. "He was shot. Twice in the chest, probably from close range, although it's hard to know exactly how close. The silencer would have blocked the gunpowder from stippling the victim's skin."

"Silencer." Casey tapped Brunelle on the arm. "That would explain why we didn't hear any gunshots."

"So would hypothermia," Brunelle pointed out.

Casey just rolled her eyes.

"A silencer, huh?" Brunelle asked. "Those are hard to come by."

"Yes." Dieter nodded. "All firearms are hard to come by in Germany. We have the strictest firearm laws in Europe."

"Is that true?" Casey asked.

Dieter shrugged. "I have not actually compared all of those laws, but I can tell you that, with very few exceptions, the private possession of firearms is very much illegal in Germany."

"Good to know," Brunelle said to Casey.

She frowned in response.

They had reached Dieter's desk. He hadn't introduced them to any of the half dozen or so other inspectors working away at their desks in the large open room. But the sound of English being spoken had drawn enough attention that several of them were looking their way.

"This is my desk," Dieter announced, placing his fingertips on the desktop. It was typical government-issue, a little nicer than Brunelle's back home actually. There was only one chair for guests, and it was on the side, in the walkway between the rows of desks. "Let me fetch another chair."

Brunelle was about to protest that he could stand, but Dieter was already grabbing the rolling chair from one workstation over. That was fine. Brunelle certainly didn't mind sitting. They'd done a lot of walking already on the trip. It was nice to follow a spa day with a sit day, even if the spa day had also been a murder day.

Once everyone was seated around Dieter's desk, he pulled out two pieces of paper from the bottom drawer.

"These are witness statement forms," he explained.

"They look just like ours," Casey noted.

"Except I can read ours," Brunelle complained. "How do I know where to put my name?"

Casey pointed at the first blank line, where the German

cognate *Name* was printed. "Where it says name," she deadpanned.

"Oh, well I can understand that," Brunelle realized, "and I suppose *Adresse* means 'address'?"

"Now you're getting the hang of it," Casey encouraged. "Only five hundred thousand more words or so and you'll speak like a native."

Brunelle ignored his girlfriend. "I'm going to have to write in English," he told Dieter. "Is that going to be all right?"

"Oh, yes. Absolutely," Dieter answered. "No one is ever going to read them anyway. I'm only bothering because Chief Inspector Leptheimer insisted."

"Well, that's good," Brunelle replied. "I guess."

Casey was less relieved. "No one's going to read them? The written statements of the first eyewitnesses? The people who found the body?"

Dieter shrugged. "The fact that the man was dead is not open to debate. The questions will be: Who made him dead? How? And why? You have no information about any of that. Feel free to write in any language you wish. Do you know Japanese? Swahili perhaps?"

"Is this a joke?" Casey asked. "Why even have us come here if there's no point to writing out a statement?"

For his part, Brunelle was relieved he wasn't going to have to fight through the form. *Geschlecht* didn't look like a cognate for any English word he could think of.

"I invited you to give you a tour of our police station," Dieter answered. "After all, would you rather be the witnesses on this case or one of the investigators?"

Casey's eyes widened. "One of the investigators? You want us to work on the case with you?"

"If you are willing," Dieter offered. "It gets boring doing things the official way all the time. What do you Americans say? Rules are meant to be broken, yes?"

Brunelle raised a hesitant finger. "I'm not actually a police officer."

"Shut up, Davey," Casey shot off without looking at Brunelle. She half stood up and leaned forward on Dieter's desk. "You're serious?"

Dieter smiled and tapped the form in front of her. "Think of this not as a witness statement but rather a detective's report."

Casey threw Brunelle a 'Can you believe this?' look, to which he responded with a 'Why, yes, this is unexpected' shrug.

"Of course, we cannot break all of the rules," Dieter was quick to clarify. "There would be legal problems for the case if you did a task which only a commissioned police officer is permitted to do."

Casey nodded as she sat down again. "Of course, of course. That only makes sense. We—I mean, you wouldn't want any evidence suppressed."

"Yes, that would be a concern," Dieter confirmed. "So, are you, as you say, in?"

Casey smiled. She didn't look to Brunelle for approval. "Oh, yeah. I'm in. What do we do first?"

Before Dieter could answer, a uniformed officer appeared and reported something to Dieter in German. Brunelle didn't understand, but it was obvious Casey did by the excited look she gave him.

"It appears my officers have located the suspect," Dieter reported. "Would you be interested in attending the questioning?"

"Yes!" Casey sprang out of her seat and scanned the

office, presumably for a door with whatever the German word for 'Interrogation' was on it. "Let's go!"

But Dieter didn't stand up. Brunelle decided to follow the German's lead.

"Why are you standing up?" Dieter asked Casey.

"To walk to the interrogation room," Casey hazarded, still scanning the room.

Dieter smiled. "The interrogation room is a courtroom," he informed them. "The questioning will be done by the public prosecutor, and perhaps the judge."

"The judge?" Brunelle was stunned.

"The prosecutor?" Casey seemed even more shocked by the thought of that. "That seems like a bad idea."

Brunelle tipped his head at her. "Really?"

"You're not a cop," Casey reminded him.

"I ask questions for a living," Brunelle defended.

"Questions you already know the answers to," Casey returned, "thanks to cops like me."

Brunelle frowned, but she had a point. One of the maxims of trial work was, 'Never ask a question you don't already know the answer to.' But he was still irritated.

"So, the prosecutor asks the questions," Casey clarified, "and you just watch?"

"Yes," Dieter confirmed. He looked at his watch. "This is a murder investigation. The public prosecutor will want to do the preliminary examination herself."

Casey frowned. "Is she any good?"

Dieter's eyebrows raised, and he laughed slightly. "Sabine Ehrenwald? Oh, yes. She's the best."

CHAPTER 4

Sabine Ehrenwald's office was in the *Staatsanwaltschaft* building, southwest of the city center, *Staatsanwalt* translating as 'state's attorney'. The exterior boasted 19th Century Romantic architecture that would have felt right at home on the Champs d'Elysee. The interior was decorated sparsely but sharply, reflecting the occupant they had come to see. Sabine Ehrenwald stood up brusquely when Dieter entered her office announced, two strangers in tow.

She was tall, very tall. Several inches taller than Brunelle, in fact. She was thin, but not frail, with muscular arms exposed by her sleeveless blouse, her suit coat hung on a wrought iron coatrack by the door. She had pale skin, with gray eyes and short black hair cut in a severe bob. Red lipstick accentuated her scowl.

She barked something at Dieter, who tried to play it off with a laugh and what sounded very much like an apology.

"She doesn't like being interrupted," Casey whispered to Brunelle.

Sabine grumbled something in reply to Dieter's supplication, throwing a glare at Brunelle and Casey.

"She doesn't like Americans either," Casey translated.

Another guttural bark at Dieter.

"And she doesn't like Dieter," Brunelle remarked. "Even I can tell that."

"Whether I like any of you is irrelevant," Sabine turned and addressed the Americans in perfect English. "Your interruption disturbs my ability to complete my work effectively and efficiently. That is relevant, and unacceptable."

Brunelle nodded for a moment, then extended his hand. "Dave—Davey Brunelle." He decided to go with it. "I'm also a prosecutor. Nice to meet you."

Sabine narrowed her eyes even further, but after a moment she shook Brunelle's hand. Her grip was a little too tight, wrapping Brunelle's hand into a bony vise. "Hello."

She released Brunelle's hand and turned her attention to Casey. "So, you are a police officer, according to Junior Inspector Vorsburg."

"I'm a detective," Casey clarified. "I believe he said as much."

Sabine's scowl curled into a tight grin. "You speak German?"

"I do." Casey nodded. She didn't mention Brunelle didn't speak a word of it. For one thing, there was no need to volunteer information. For another, Brunelle would make it obvious enough soon enough.

"I don't." Brunelle raised a finger in the air. That was quick. "English is fine by me."

Sabine didn't even try to suppress her eye roll and disgusted sigh. "Of course," she groaned. "Whatever we can do to make your stay more enjoyable. You are leaving soon, I hope?"

Brunelle was a bit taken aback by Sabine's increasing

rudeness. Casey took it as a challenge.

"No, actually," Casey said. "In fact, we're thinking of extending our stay."

That was the first Brunelle had heard of that, but he knew not to contradict his girlfriend, at least not right then.

"They are interested in the Balibai murder," Dieter explained. "They were there the night the murder was committed."

"You are witnesses?" Sabine asked. "To a murder? I should say you'll be extending your stay."

"Not witnesses exactly," Dieter claimed. "They didn't see the murder. They were simply there at closing time when the body was discovered."

By us, Brunelle thought. But again, he kept his mouth shut.

"Ms. Emory is a police detective," Dieter went on, "and Mr. Brunelle is a prosecutor on murder cases. This is wonderful opportunity to learn about each other's practices regarding criminal investigations and prosecution."

"To what end?" Sabine scoffed. "Police work is police work," she dismissed Dieter and Casey—the cops. Moving on to Brunelle, she said, "And our trials are very different from the American circus trials we see on the news. There are no juries to trick with ill-fitting gloves and ridiculous rhymes. No, I see no value in this exchange."

"We only want to observe," Casey assured her. "You won't even know we're there."

"I know you are here, now," Sabine sniffed. "That is bad enough. I do not need two foreigners sitting in the courtroom, whispering likely inaccurate translations while I examine a murderer."

"Accused murderer," Brunelle decided to jump in, even if only to irritate Sabine. A simple enough task, actually.

"Suspects are not presumed innocent here, Mr. Brunelle," Sabine hissed. "We try not to arrest innocent people. Another difference between our systems, I think."

Brunelle was tempted to bring things to a head by inquiring whether Germany had an open courtroom rule, like back home in Seattle. If so, Sabine couldn't prevent them from observing even if she wanted to. However, if they didn't have that rule, and he reminded Sabine of that, then they were done, and she had won. Luckily, Sabine filled the silence before he had to decide whether to say anything.

She let out a loud sigh and threw a narrow-eyed dagger glare at Dieter. Then she turned and pointed at Casey. "No translating," she demanded. "No whispering. No words at all."

Casey took a moment, then nodded. No words.

Sabine swung her index finger to Brunelle. "And you. If you don't understand the proceeding, then you suffer through it, or you wait outside in the hall. Agreed?"

Brunelle looked to Casey, who nodded again. He turned back to Sabine. "Agreed."

Sabine sighed again and dropped herself back into her chair.

The negotiations concluded, Casey bubbled up again. "So, when do we start?"

Sabine frowned. "*I* start," she emphasized, "the first court day after the arrest. Therefore, your question might better be directed to *Kommissaranwärter* Vorsburg."

All eyes turned to Dieter. But he simply smiled and shrugged. "They only told me the suspect had been located. I don't know when he will be arrested. Maybe today. Probably today. Tomorrow at the latest." He paused. "Maybe the next day."

Sabine and Casey both frowned.

"Right." Dieter gestured vaguely toward the hallway and the world outside Sabine Ehrenwald's office. "I'll find out."

"Do," Sabine instructed, "and I will, unfortunately, see all of you the day after that."

CHAPTER 5

As it turned out, the arrest had been made while Sabine was playing gracious hostess to Dieter and his American companions. The suspect was a new employee at Spa Balibai. His name was Mathias Ginkel. It just sounded guilty.

"How do you know what sounds guilty in German?" Casey cocked her head at Brunelle over her plate of gnocchi.

They hadn't had time to think out their lunch plans, and it was well after noon by the time they left the Berlin Public Prosecutor's headquarters, so they found the nearest Italian restaurant and ducked inside. There were a lot of Italian restaurants in Berlin, and they all featured excellent food at reasonable prices. Plus beer and wine.

"Ginkel?" Brunelle repeated the name for her. "That sounds like what you would call someone who ratted out the rest of the gang. 'That Mathias, he's such a ginkel. Told the cops everything.'"

"Wouldn't that make him not guilty?" Casey questioned. "If he's ratting out the other people who are really guilty?"

"He was in on it too," Brunelle explained. "He's just

trying to get a deal. Fucking ginkel."

"Well, maybe that's what will happen tomorrow," Casey suggested. "Maybe he'll crack under the withering questioning of Public Prosecutor Sabine Ehrenwald. Full confession. Give up his whole gang. She'll bring down one of Berlin's largest criminal organizations in a single examination."

Brunelle laughed but then shrugged. "Not that I would know. You aren't allowed to translate for me."

"Well, not right then and there," Casey agreed. "But I can give you a summary afterward."

Brunelle shrugged again, but this time paired it with a slight frown. "Not quite the same. But I'll take what I can get."

Casey's own face unfurled a smile. "Well, there is another option."

Brunelle thought for a moment, even as his surprisingly large glass of red wine was beginning to blur his cognition a bit. "Maybe Ginkel speaks English?"

Casey shook her head at him. "No, silly. I'm sure the official proceedings will all be in German. The judge is definitely going to speak German. And even if everyone else were speaking English, Sabine would stay in German just to spite us."

"Spite me," Brunelle pointed at her with his fork.

"Right," Casey agreed. "Spite you. So, why even come to the examination at all?"

Brunelle's frown returned. "You want me to stay back at the hotel while you play detective?"

"No," Casey assured him. "I want you to play detective while I play lawyer."

Brunelle shook his head at her. "What are you talking about?"

Casey leaned forward. "Look, there's no point to you

coming to the examination, except maybe to see what Ginkel looks like. After that, you'll just sit there, dying to whisper to me for a whispered-back translation, and then, when I finally give in, we both get kicked out, which is the worst possible result."

Brunelle wanted to argue, but she knew him too well.

"So, instead of ruining everything," she said as kindly as she could, "why don't you make up some excuse to talk with Dieter about the case? Go find a place in the courthouse. Or grab coffee nearby. Aren't you curious about how they identified Ginkel? How the arrest went down? Do they really not ask any questions until the next day?—which is crazy by the way."

"That is crazy," Brunelle agreed. "Why give the suspect an entire day to consider whether to answer questions?"

"Right?"

"Probably so he can decide whether to be a ginkel," Brunelle posited before taking another sip of wine.

Casey rolled her eyes. "Yeah, sure, whatever. If that's what it takes to find out more about the case, then sure, go with the ginkel angle. I'm sure Dieter will love it when you make fun of his language and culture."

Brunelle considered for a moment. "I don't know. He seems pretty cool. He might think it's funny."

"Yeah, you're right," Casey laughed. "So, you go find out all that while I watch Sabine grill the suspect. In a public courtroom. With a judge present. And probably a nice glass of cool water to sip from. Maybe a neck rub."

"It does seem silly," Brunelle agreed. "But I guess it's just different."

"How tolerant of you," Casey admired.

"Whatever." Brunelle shrugged it off. "I'm just happy I get the better part of the bargain."

Casey raised an eyebrow. "How so?"

"I get to spend the morning with Dieter," Brunelle pointed out. "You're stuck with Sabine."

CHAPTER 6

First thing the next morning found Brunelle and Casey entering Berlin's criminal courthouse, *Kriminalgericht*, mixed in with the morning crush of courthouse employees reporting to work. The examination of Mathias Ginkel was assigned to a Judge Frist, whose chambers they located on the third floor. Brunelle had packed one suit in case they decided to go out to a fancy dinner. Unfortunately for Casey, her equivalent to Brunelle's suit was a slinky yellow dress—not exactly court attire. That discrepancy had led to a shopping trip the previous afternoon to Berlin's famous Kurfürstendamm Street in the upscale Charlottenburg District. Followed by an actual purchase of a simple gray suit at the Potsdamer Platz mall for a third of the price. But the cafés on Kurfürstendamm Street were very nice.

When they arrived at the courtroom, they found Dieter waiting outside. Sabine, Brunelle felt confident, was already inside.

"Casey! Davey! You made it," Dieter called out. "I'm so glad."

"We wouldn't miss it for the world," Casey replied.

Except Brunelle was absolutely planning on missing it. And making Dieter miss it too.

Dieter's expression turned serious. "Remember the rules. No whispering translations. No whispering anything. We do not want to distract Sabine during her examination."

"Yeah, about that…" Brunelle started. "I'm not sure what good it will do for me to sit through a bunch of testimony I don't understand. Especially if I can't get any help from Casey."

"Good point, Davey," Casey put in, only a little bit rehearsed.

"So, I was thinking," Brunelle went on, "maybe you and I could go somewhere and talk about the facts of the case. You know, brief me on what we know so far. Is there a good coffee shop nearby?"

"What? No," Dieter answered. "I mean, yes, there are many good cafés nearby. But no, I can't leave the courthouse. This is the preliminary examination of a murder suspect. I need to be present in the courtroom to hear his testimony firsthand and enter it into the reports."

Brunelle frowned. Another glance to Casey, but for direction instead of correction.

"Besides," Dieter went on. "Even if you can't understand all of the words spoken—"

"Any," Brunelle interrupted. "Any of the words said."

"Yes, good," Dieter agreed. "Even if you can't understand any of the words said, there is other information to be gathered from seeing the suspect, judging his age and appearance, observing his mannerisms as he answers difficult questions. Yes, you can learn a lot about a person from how they present themselves, especially under pressure."

Another glance at Casey. She shrugged. Dieter did have a

point. And Brunelle was interested in what Matty the Ginkel looked like. He imagined an overweight, pasty, sweaty, blob of a man. Spineless. The kind of guy who ginkels his buddies to the cops.

"Fine," Brunelle sighed. He pointed at the bundle under Dieter's arm. "But can I at least look at the file while he's talking? Something to do so I'm not tempted to beg you guys for the occasional translation?"

Dieter looked down at the file. "It is all in German," he protested.

Brunelle shrugged again. "Maybe I'll learn a few more words. Like *Name* and *Adresse*. Who knows? Maybe I'll be fluent by the end of the hearing."

"That seems unlikely," Dieter opined. He handed Brunelle the case file. "But I see no harm. Good luck."

Brunelle took the file and thanked Dieter. Then the three of them entered the courtroom. They tried to be as silent as possible, but even the quietest entrance was enough to draw Sabine's attention—and ire. She spun her face at them, but only long enough to scowl and nod sharply at the seats in the gallery. Then she turned back to the materials spread across the prosecutor's table. There was no one at the defense attorney table, and the judge hadn't taken the bench yet,

The courtroom looked roughly the same as any courtroom back in the United States, Brunelle observed. The décor was classic dark wood with cream accent walls. There was a raised dais for the judge to sit, although it was wider than he was used to. He remembered something about there sometimes being panels of judges, even for trials. Below the judges' seats were court staff, already in the courtroom and busy at whatever work they needed to do to prepare for the hearing. A single

uniformed guard stood by a door to one side. Brunelle guessed
that was where the suspect would be brought in, likely by another
uniformed guard or two. Other than that, the courtroom was
empty.

Dieter pointed to the last row of the gallery. "Let us sit in
the back." He looked at Brunelle. "Just in case you cannot control
your desire to whisper."

Brunelle raised the case file, then pulled an imaginary
zipper across his lips.

Casey smiled and patted him on the shoulder. "I'll
translate it all for you after the hearing."

Brunelle nodded, but still didn't say anything. His lips
were zipped shut after all.

He opened the case file and began flipping through the
first few pages. Sure enough, it was all in German. He sighed.

After a few minutes, the judge entered the courtroom.
Brunelle instinctively stood up, then wondered whether that was
also the custom there. Casey followed suit, as did Dieter,
although again Brunelle wondered whether Dieter was just
following their lead. Sabine was already standing; she addressed
some sort of greeting to the judge as he sat down.

He was in his fifties, Brunelle guessed, with black hair
graying at the temples. His face was thin, with deep wrinkles
running down either side of his face, already sporting a five
o'clock shadow first thing in the morning.

He said something in German with a crisp baritone, and
people started moving around, most importantly the guard by
the door, who unlocked said door and allowed one of his
colleagues to enter the courtroom, Mathias Ginkel in tow.

Brunelle had expected jail jammies and handcuffs. He'd
also expected a weak-looking middle-aged lump of a man—

although he realized that was based on the man's name, not his crime. Instead, however, Mathias Ginkel was a skinny teenager, no handcuffs, and in a navy blue outfit that wouldn't have looked out of place on the street outside. He was pale and gaunt, with bags under his eyes and an unkempt mop of black hair atop his narrow head. His ears were a bit too big, as was his Adam's apple, but his shoulders were too narrow. Large hands and larger feet finished the look of a very awkward, and very young man.

A very awkward young murderer, that is.

More German from the judge, and Ginkel was escorted to what appeared to be the witness stand, off to one side and facing the judge's bench. Once he was seated, two things happened: the guards took up positions on either side of him, and Brunelle stood up and walked out of the courtroom.

It was painfully obvious he wasn't going to understand one damn thing that happened in there. But he'd accomplished the two goals he'd set for himself when he entered the courtroom. The first was to see and size up Mathias Ginkel.

The second was to find the page in Dieter's file that listed Ginkel's *Name* and *Adresse*. He had somewhere to go for the morning after all.

CHAPTER 7

Mathias Ginkel's listed *Adresse* was Baumstrasse 1345. Brunelle's smartphone had no trouble locating it, and the Berlin U-Bahn app they'd downloaded upon their arrival told him exactly how to get there. But it didn't prepare him for what he saw when he emerged from the subway station into the middle of Mathias Ginkel's neighborhood.

Up to that point in their trip, Brunelle and Casey had spent their time in Berlin's nicer districts. The shopping district of Charlottenburg, the tourist-rich downtown *Mitte*, the famous Alexanderplatz. Brunelle had no idea what Ginkel's neighborhood was called, but he knew it wasn't famous, there were no tourists, and the only shopping was from the small rundown grocery store he spied from the top of the subway stairs and whatever people were selling on the street.

And there were a lot of people on the street just then. It was all the more noticeable because they were people of working age, mostly men, and yet none of them were at work midmorning on a weekday. Although Brunelle suspected the commercial transactions likely taking place just out of sight were definitely a source of income. Speaking of work, he suddenly became very aware that he was wearing a business suit. It would have been hard to look more out of place. He came to an abrupt stop, leading the person behind him to bump into him at the top of the stairs, as Brunelle blocked the exit, stunned and agog at the desperately poor neighborhood he unexpectedly found himself in.

"*Blah blah blah!*" the large, burly man seemed to yell, glaring at him over large, broad shoulders.

Brunelle shrugged, smiled, and waved at the man in a way that he hoped conveyed his apologies. The man had already turned back to face whatever way he was going. Brunelle decided to start walking himself, lest the next person who had to push past him not be as understanding.

Brunelle hurried across a small island in the middle of the street and crossed at the crosswalk to that rundown grocery store he'd spotted. He pulled out the scrap of paper he'd scribbled Ginkel's address down on and scanned the area to get his bearings. The street sign at the corner said Baumstrasse. So he was already halfway there. He just needed to find 1345. Checking the numbers above the grocery store's entrance and the one on the business next door, Brunelle determined he was on the correct side of the street, but a few blocks away still. He lowered his head, pretended to ignore the increasing number of people staring at him, and began his march up Baumstrasse.

He didn't get far.

"Hey!" a man's voice called out after him. He was pretty sure it meant the same thing in German as it did in English. "*Hey, Du!*"

Hey you! Brunelle could guess. He considered ignoring the person, but decided it was probably better to face whoever might be about to attack him. He stopped and turned around.

The man who had called out after him was probably about

the same age as Mathias Ginkel, that is, barely a man at all. He was short, but with thick arms and thicker eyebrows, a shaved head, and an angry yet cocky expression on his face.

He barked a question at Brunelle, but of course Brunelle didn't understand.

Brunelle pointed at himself and grasped at a couple of words from that phrase Casey had taught him. *"Deutsch nicht,"* he tried. "No German. English?"

Brunelle had been assured more than once—mostly by Casey—that everyone in Germany spoke at least a little bit of English. However, his experience had been that, generally speaking, the higher one's station and the more likely one had gone to college ('university'), the more likely the person was to be able to actually speak English. The young man in front of him looked neither high-stationed nor college-educated. Brunelle's question seemed only to remind them both of that fact.

The man yelled something back at him, and Brunelle could make out the words *'Englisch'* and *'Deutschland'* in it. He could discern the man's general complaint about some foreigner coming into his country, his neighborhood, and not even speaking the language. Brunelle could hardly disagree. Then again, he hadn't asked to be accosted by the young man. Everything would have been fine if he had simply let Brunelle complete his task in peace.

Which gave Brunelle an idea. Maybe if they had a common goal.

He held up the scrap of paper with 'Baumstrasse 1345' written on it. He didn't know how to ask where it was, but he could, and did, point at it and grunt in a way that sounded like a question.

The angry young man squinted at the paper, then seemed

to become at least a little bit less angry. Which was a relief because several other somewhat angry young men, and a couple of angry-looking young women, were starting to make their way over.

Finally, after a few moments and several of the oncoming crowd arriving at their location, the young man asked, "Mathias?"

Brunelle smiled and nodded, both a bit exaggeratedly. "*Ja.*" He knew that word too. "Mathias."

Unfortunately, whatever the man said next was completely lost on Brunelle. But it didn't seem lost on the assembled crowd of ne'er-do-well urchins. There was a lot of chatter, the name Mathias repeated several times, and a general tone of concern.

Two of the girls stepped forward, one with green hair, the other with blue; they looked even younger than the rest. The heavy eye makeup on the blue one couldn't hide the fear in her eyes, and the tight shirt on her belly really couldn't hide that she was very, very pregnant. The black lipstick on the green-haired girl parted to speak, finally, at least some English.

"Where is Mathias?" she asked competently enough. She pointed at blue girl. "This is his girlfriend. Where is he? We do not know where he is gone."

Apparently, Mathias was part of the Baumstrasse no-job crew. Or at least, he worked nights, freeing up his days to hang out with the best and brightest the future of Berlin had to offer.

"Um..." Brunelle hesitated. This wasn't going to help matters. "He was arrested."

He expected a bad reaction, but it only prompted a confused expression on his translator's face. She probably didn't know that particular phrase. He took a moment to remember that other word Casey had taught him when they were discussing the

merits of trespassing overnight at Spa Balibai. Then he offered it
up. "*Gefängnis*." Jail.

"*Gefängnis?!*" blue girlfriend wailed. She dropped to her
knees and started sobbing. The assembled crowd split evenly
between bending down to console her and stepping forward to
menace Brunelle.

"I didn't do it." Brunelle raised his palms at his
aggressors. "I just—I just wanted to look around where he lived.
I thought…" But he trailed off. He wasn't sure anymore what he
thought he would accomplish. Getting a better feel for their
suspect, he supposed. At least that was working out, after a
fashion.

"Why is he in, um, *Gefängnis*?" Green asked. "Who are
you?"

"Um…" This wasn't going to help either. He hoped it was
a cognate, because he definitely didn't know the word in German.
"Murder."

"Murder," the translator repeated, her eyes widening.
Guess she knew that word well enough. "*Mord!*"

It is a cognate, Brunelle noted absently.

Girlfriend looked up at Brunelle long enough to repeat the
word. "*Mord.*" Her eyes looked sad. But not surprised.

Brunelle had been interested in seeing Mathias's home.
He wanted to get a feel for the man. He decided he'd
accomplished that goal, and it was probably time to get back to
the courthouse and the hell out of whatever marginalized
neighborhood he found himself in. But he didn't have to be a jerk
about it.

He bent down, too, and put a hand on blue girlfriend's
shoulder. He didn't know the German phrase, but he guessed
they might know the English word. "Sorry," he said.

"Who are you?" Green asked again. "How do you know this?"

"A lawyer sent me," Brunelle mostly lied. He was the lawyer who sent himself. "You should go see Mathias. He's in big trouble."

The others didn't seem to understand that particular phrase either, but the news itself seemed to stun everyone enough that he was able to start walking away without being further accosted.

He started backwards so he could keep an eye on any potential pursuers, but they were just watching him, or directing their attention to Mathias's pregnant girlfriend.

"*Hey, Du,*" the original angry young man called out again. But the anger was gone from his face. "*Danke.* Thank you."

Brunelle didn't know the word for 'You're welcome.' Instead he just nodded and waved one last time.

Then he got the hell out of there.

CHAPTER 8

"You did what?" Casey nearly shouted at him when he finally found her in the lobby of the courthouse—nowhere near Judge Frist's courtroom. "I thought you went back to the hotel bar or something. No wonder you didn't answer your phone."

"Hotel bar?" Brunelle protested. "It was like nine in the morning."

"Whatever." Casey waved his protest away. "Why the hell would you go to his house?"

"I'm pretty sure I was going to an apartment," Brunelle observed. "Although I never made it that far. Still, apartment, not house."

"I don't care if it was a fucking castle," Casey said. "Why didn't you just hang around or something? It took like fifteen minutes."

"I couldn't understand a damn word," Brunelle defended. Then, "Wait, it only took fifteen minutes? Why?"

Casey took a long, deep breath. "Sounds like we each have a lot to tell the other. Why don't we go to that hotel bar and debrief?"

"Should we find Dieter?" Brunelle suggested. "Not

Sabine, though, right?"

"Definitely not Sabine," Casey agreed. "But I'm not sure about Dieter either. He seemed kind of put out when you disappeared. Why don't you tell me exactly how you compromised his investigation before we talk with him again?"

Brunelle crossed his arms. "I feel like you don't trust me."

"I trust you," Casey assured him. "I trust you messed up his case, or part of it anyway. Come on," she grabbed his arm and slipped hers around it. "Let's go see how bad you screwed up."

* * *

"Wow, that's really bad," Casey appraised after Brunelle told her the story.

"What I did," Brunelle asked, "or what I learned?"

They were back near their hotel, but not quite there and not at a bar. There was a Thai restaurant around the corner and by the time they got back to their district and off the subway, it was past lunchtime. Berlin had a lot of Thai restaurants too, and they were also excellent. It was their third trip to that particular one.

"Both," Casey answered, as the waiter set down two glasses of water and a plate of spring rolls, "but in different ways. I guess we don't know very much about this case after all. He's got a pregnant girlfriend?"

"Pregnant teenage girlfriend," Brunelle expounded. "Although he doesn't look like much more than a teenager himself."

"He's nineteen," Casey confirmed. "They started the hearing with his name and date of birth. I was surprised by how young he looked, so I paid attention to that."

"I was surprised too," Brunelle said. "He seems awful young to just kill some guy at the spa where he worked. Judging by his friends, he might have been the only one with a job, even if it was nights folding towels. What did he say at the examination?"

"That's just it." Casey shrugged. "He didn't say anything. After he identified himself, but before Sabine could ask any questions, the judge advised him of a bunch of rights. Similar to ours, but not quite the same. The judge told him he had the right to have an attorney present for the examination, and he didn't have to answer any questions, although if he chose to answer some but not others, his refusal to answer certain questions could be used against him."

"That's interesting," Brunelle remarked.

"Yeah, I thought you'd think so," Casey replied. "But it was mostly just irritating, because after the judge said all that, Ginkel sat there for a few seconds, then said he didn't want to answer any questions at all, and he wanted a lawyer."

"That's why they should have interrogated him at the time of arrest," Brunelle said. "Before he had time to think about everything."

"Well, now, see, that's the interesting part." Casey pointed a half-eaten spring roll at her boyfriend. "Apparently, you don't actually have to wait until the next court day to do the interrogation."

"Examination," Brunelle corrected.

"Well, right. Exactly," Casey answered. "The examination is what the prosecutor does in court, and that does have to be the next court day. But there's nothing actually preventing the cops from talking to the suspect earlier than that. Like, at the time of arrest."

"When he's scared and most likely to try to talk his way out of it with some lie that can be easily disproved," Brunelle knew.

"And get caught in the lie, then confess." Casey knew it too.

"So why didn't Dieter interrogate Ginkel when he was arrested?"

"That's the question, isn't it?" Casey popped the last of the spring roll into her mouth.

Brunelle picked one up too, but didn't bite into it yet. "Who has the answer? Dieter? Sabine? That big mean cop who yelled at Dieter? Leppensomething?"

"His boss?" Casey confirmed. "Leptheimer, I think." She thought some more. "Maybe. Sabine probably doesn't know."

"I bet Leppenheimer doesn't know either," Brunelle opined. "If Dieter screwed up, he seems more like the kind of guy to cover it up than ask for help."

"Kind of like Mathias Ginkel," Casey observed.

Brunelle nodded his head, trying to decide what their next step should be. His thoughts were interrupted by the arrival of the Pad Thai and Prik King. Once the waiter had set down their plates and departed, Brunelle offered his opinion.

"I think I know who we should talk to," he said.

"Me too," Casey agreed.

"Dieter," she said at the same time Brunelle said, "Sabine."

Casey laughed. "Let's just ask Dieter why he didn't question the suspect at the time of arrest. That's the most direct way."

"And if it was a mistake, it's the most likely way to provide inaccurate information."

"You mean, you think he'll lie."

Brunelle shrugged. "I bet he didn't interrogate Ginkel

because Sabine ordered him not to. She seems like a control freak. A scary control freak. Didn't Dieter say something about that?"

Casey shrugged, a fork full of Prik King in her mouth. "I dunno.," she finally managed to mumble. "Maybe. I didn't realize it would be a big deal at the time."

Brunelle finished a bite of food too, then wiped his mouth with a cloth napkin. "Me neither, and maybe it's not. But let me talk with Sabine. You know, prosecutor to prosecutor."

Casey set down her fork and raised an eyebrow. "Prosecutor to prosecutor?"

Brunelle nodded. "Yeah."

"And the fact that she's super hot in an angry, spider who's going to eat you after mind-blowing sex, kind of way has nothing to do with it?" Casey challenged with a grin.

Brunelle shook his head. "Nope. Not my type. I do not want to be eaten after sex."

"You know there's a dirty joke in there, right?" Casey laughed.

"I know no such thing, madam," Brunelle insisted with faux umbrage. "I only know that I fully expect to still be alive tomorrow, after mind-blowing sex with you tonight, to ask Sabine Ehrenwald if she ordered Dieter not to interrogate a murder suspect."

Casey leaned back in her chair and crossed her arms. "You're pretty confident about all that, are you?"

Brunelle shrugged and winked at her. "I don't know about confident," he answered. "But I am hopeful."

CHAPTER 9

The night went pretty much as Brunelle had planned. So, he was in an especially good mood when he walked back into the *Staatsanwaltschaft* the next morning and asked whether Public Prosecutor Sabine Ehrenwald was in her office and available for an unexpected visitor.

Well, first he asked if the receptionist spoke English, which she did. Then he asked all that.

The receptionist made a phone call, then informed Brunelle of the answers. Yes, Sabine was in, but no she wasn't taking unscheduled visitors.

"Tell her it's that American prosecutor," Brunelle advised the receptionist. "Tell her I have new information about the Balibai murder. Tell her I spoke to some witnesses."

He knew that last part would get Sabine's attention. Not because she would want to hear what Brunelle had learned, but because she would want to yell at him for interfering with the case. He wagered her desire to correct and dominate everyone around her would be the key to her office. And maybe more.

He was right.

And she was furious.

He could see it on her face as she stormed out into the lobby, her porcelain face splotching red in anger.

"What do you think you are doing?" she bellowed. "Who do you think you are? How dare you come to my country, my city, and interfere in my prosecution of the most serious of crimes? If you have compromised my ability to hold a murderer to account for his heinous actions, I will have you charged with interfering in an official investigation, tampering with witnesses, contempt of court, and anything else I can think of. You will be extending your stay far more that you originally planned and far more than you will want, I can assure you of that."

Brunelle remained calm throughout Sabine's tirade, a reassuring smile resting gently on his lips. "I think I may have misspoken to your receptionist. My German isn't particularly good, if you recall."

"Your German is nonexistent," Sabine clipped.

"Which makes it downright terrible," Brunelle agreed. "Perhaps we could go inside to your office, and I can tell you something I discovered while out for a walk down on Baumstrasse."

One of Sabine's eyebrows shot up, but she didn't say anything. She seemed like one of those rare people who can remember everything they've ever read. She almost certainly knew Mathias Ginkel's residence was on Baumstrasse.

The truth was, Sabine was never going to agree to meet with him to answer his questions. But she might enjoy making him answer hers.

"It won't take very long," he assured her. Not something he liked having to assure admittedly beautiful women. But work was work.

Sabine stared down at him for several seconds. Then several seconds more. She was already taller than him, and even more so in the high heeled boots she was sporting that day. His neck was starting to hurt when she finally spun on one of those high heels and huffed, "Fine!" over her shoulder as she marched back toward her office. "I will give you five minutes. I have no more time than that for you, Mr. Brunelle."

Brunelle grinned to himself and followed after her. "Call me Davey."

* * *

Once they were inside Sabine's office, she was nothing but business.

"Tell me what you did," she commanded. "Tell me everything."

"Well, I'm not really sure it's all that important," Brunelle demurred. "I was wondering whether maybe you could tell me what happened this morning in court first."

Sabine narrowed her eyes. "Your girlfriend will have already told you that. The defendant refused to answer questions."

"Oh no," Brunelle leaned forward. "No, I hadn't heard that. Is that common here in Germany?"

"It is not uncommon," Sabine answered, "and I find it very unlikely your detective girlfriend has not already told you all this. She was present for the entire interaction, as was Junior Inspector Vorsburg."

"Right, right," Brunelle nodded his head. "I left after a couple of minutes. I couldn't understand anything that was going on."

"Due at least in part," Sabine cut, "to your language inabilities."

"So, Dieter—I mean, Junior Inspector Vorsburg," Brunelle corrected himself to mirror her level of formality, "was he there to see if the suspect's story changed from when he interrogated him right after the arrest?"

Sabine didn't reply right away. She sat up a bit straighter in her chair, crossed her arms, then exhaled deeply through her nose, nostrils flaring. Finally, she uncrossed her arms. "Junior Inspector Vorsburg did not interrogate Mr. Ginkel at the time of Mr. Ginkel's arrest. But," she narrowed her bright eyes at him, "I think you knew that."

Brunelle leaned back, slouched a little more into his chair, and crossed his legs. "No, no, I didn't realize that. I mean, he didn't talk about the suspect saying anything to him, but I guess I just thought he wasn't sharing all the details of the investigation. Back in the States, at least my part of the States, the suspect always gets interrogated immediately after arrest. Is that just different here? Can you ever interrogate a suspect at the time of arrest? If so, who makes that call? Him or you?"

Sabine sat stock still for several seconds. Then she frowned at him and asked, "Are you done attempting to interrogate me now, Mr. Brunelle?"

Brunelle leaned up in his seat again, uncrossing his legs. "I told you, call me Davey," he began, "and no, I'm not interrogating anyone. I'm just really curious about how your system works. Who does what. How decisions are made. Why a murder suspect would be given the night to think about whether or not he really wanted to confess. Stuff like that."

Another cold few seconds from Sabine as she considered what to say next. Brunelle wasn't sure, but it seemed like she hadn't blinked since they'd arrived in her office.

"What did you want to tell me about witnesses, Mr.

Brunelle?" she said, her red lips barely parting. "Witnesses on Baumstrasse where Mathias Ginkel lives."

"Is that where he lives?" Brunelle slapped his knee. "You know what?" He pointed at her. "That makes sense now. See, I was flipping through Dieter—I mean, Junior Inspector Vorsburg's case file when I saw this one German word I know, '*Adresse*'—I don't know how to pronounce it actually."

"No, you don't," Sabine confirmed. "Why were you looking at an official police file, if I might ask?"

"I was bored," Brunelle answered. "I couldn't understand anything, remember? Besides, you said Casey—I mean, Detective Emory wasn't allowed to translate for me. Well, I was thinking maybe I'd go back to the spa, maybe get a massage or something, you know? Well, when I saw the word '*Adresse*', I thought that meant the address where the crime occurred. You know, the address for Spa Balibai. So, I ducked out and took the U-Bahn there. But when I got there, I didn't recognize anything because, of course, I was in the wrong place."

"Is there a point to this lie, Mr. Brunelle?" Sabine inquired stone-faced.

"No, no lies, Sabine." Brunelle clicked his tongue at himself. "I mean Public Prosecutor Ehrenwald. No lies. I was walking up Baumstrasse, and I heard some kids talking and one of them started crying. It turns out she's Mathias Ginkel's girlfriend and she's pregnant."

"And they were all speaking English for your benefit, I assume?" That eyebrow of Sabine's went up again.

"No, no, it was all in German," Brunelle assured her. "But I didn't need to speak German to see her belly. Or the tears."

Sabine frowned at him, although she was already frowning, so she frowned more deeply at him.

"So, there it is," Brunelle concluded. "That's it. I thought you might want to know. Maybe you could use it as leverage on him or something."

"First of all, our rules of criminal procedure prohibit me from using leverage against a defendant," Sabine explained. "Second of all, do you mean to tell me that you came all the way down here to lie about why you were snooping around the defendant's residence, in the hopes I would tell you whether I ordered Junior Inspector Vorsburg not to interrogate the defendant prior to my formal examination?"

Brunelle had to hand it to her. She saw right through him.

"Maybe," he admitted. "Did you tell him that?"

She ignored the question. Instead she looked toward her open door and shouted, "Kaufmann!" A uniformed police officer appeared in her doorway. She gave him an order in German, but Brunelle knew the gist of it. He stood up even as Officer Kaufmann placed a grip on his shoulder.

"Nice talking with you," Brunelle offered.

Sabine didn't answer at all. She was done with him.

CHAPTER 10

As soon as Brunelle stepped out of the *Staatsanwaltschaft*, he pulled out his phone and called Casey.

"You were right," he said when she answered. "Sabine didn't tell me anything."

"That's okay," Casey answered. "I was right twice. I'm with Dieter right now, and he's telling me everything."

Brunelle halted his gait. "What? I thought we agreed to let me talk to Sabine first?"

"We did," Casey confirmed. "And you did. Now get back to the hotel before Dieter's done talking."

"That might be a while," Brunelle joked.

Casey laughed. "Hurry anyway."

* * *

'Back to the hotel' actually meant 'back to the café next door to the hotel but connected to the hotel lobby via an inside doorway.' They weren't about to discuss an open murder investigation in a hotel lobby where everyone would overhear. Much better was a busy café where no one would be listening to anything but their own conversations.

Brunelle walked in through the lobby and started scanning the crowded coffee shop for Casey.

"Dave!" she called out from a corner table. "Over here."

"Dave?" Brunelle heard Dieter ask her as he zigzagged through the other patrons. "I thought it was Davey."

"Oh, um, it is," Casey assured him. "He hates it when I call him 'Dave'. I'm just teasing him."

"Ah." Dieter forced a laugh. "Ok."

"Sure," Brunelle agreed as he sat down at the tiny table. "Caysums and Davey."

"Caysums?" Dieter looked confused.

"Don't even try, Davey." Casey shook her head at Brunelle. "You'll never keep up with me."

Brunelle frowned, but figured she was probably right. "Then let me keep up, or catch up, with Dieter here. What have we learned this morning, apart from the fact that Sabine Ehrenwald has no heart?"

"I don't know about that," Dieter replied. "But she does have an iron fist." Then he frowned slightly. "That is the phrase, correct? Iron fist. Very much in control, yes?"

"Yes," Brunelle assured him. "She is very much in control. We have other words for that too."

Casey narrowed her eyes at him.

"But those other words are very unfair," Brunelle was quick to amend. "So, let's stick with iron fist. Strong and fair. Tall, dark, and mysterious."

Casey's eyes narrowed even further. "Oh, really?"

Brunelle raised his palms defensively. "You know what? I'm going to stop talking. Dieter, why don't you talk? I would love it if you were the one who was talking. Please, talk."

Dieter smirked at the romantic drama unfolding around

him. He knew to look to Casey. "Shall I talk?"

Casey nodded, one eye still on her boyfriend. "I think that would be a good idea."

Dieter sat up a bit and cleared his throat. "All right then. So, Casey—Caysums?" A frown from her. "No, Casey—Casey asked me why I didn't interrogate Mathias Ginkel the night he was arrested."

"Why didn't you?" Brunelle prompted.

"Because Sabine ordered me not to," Dieter explained. "Ordinarily I would have, of course. It is a murder case, yes? That is why I would want to talk to him as soon as he is arrested. But that is also why I listened to Sabine and did what she told me to. It was too important not to follow the directive of the public prosecutor."

Brunelle leaned back and rubbed his chin. "I wish my detectives gave me that kind of respect."

"Respect is earned, honey." Casey patted him on the knee. "Keep working on it."

Brunelle smiled at the joke, but continued. "Is it normal for a public prosecutor to direct your investigation?"

Dieter thought for a moment. "It is not unusual. It depends very much on the nature of the case. I would be surprised if a prosecutor contacted me about, say, a case of theft. But a case of murder? No, that is not surprising."

Brunelle frowned. "It still seems strange to me."

"Foreign?" Casey suggested. "Yeah, it is foreign. That's kind of the whole point."

Brunelle offered a sarcastic, "Ha ha," then realized something. "How did you even catch him? How did you identify Ginkel as the murderer?"

"Ah yes," Dieter nodded. "He was on the spa's security

video."

Brunelle raised his eyebrows. "You have the murder on video? No wonder Sabine told you not to bother interrogating the suspect."

Dieter shook his head. "No, not the murder. That happened in the dark, outside, after the lights were turned off. All you can see is a flash between two of the sauna buildings, right by the cold plunge pool where the body was found. But Ginkel is seen on video exiting the building right by those sauna buildings, just before the gunshots."

"Does the video capture him putting the body in the cold plunge pool?" Brunelle asked.

"Not exactly." Dieter shrugged. "It appears our victim stumbled backward into the pool after being shot. A few moments later, Ginkel reenters the spa building and hurries out a side door."

"Sounds pretty solid to me," Casey said.

"Sounds pretty circumstantial to me." Brunelle frowned again.

"Murder cases usually are circumstantial," Casey countered. "Most people don't commit murder in front of witnesses. And the only other person who could tell you what happened is dead."

Brunelle thought for a moment, then realized something. "Who was the victim anyway?"

"You don't know?" Dieter's eyes widened. "But of course not. You are visitors. The victim was Viktor Ferensz, the owner of Berlin's most successful cabaret club."

"Cabaret, huh?" Casey raised an eyebrow and unfurled a smile at her boyfriend. "Looks like tonight is date night."

CHAPTER 11

Of course, every night was date night while on vacation. Brunelle was getting more use out of that one suit he'd brought than he'd expected. And Casey finally got to wear that yellow evening dress she'd brought. They pulled up short when they turned the corner and found themselves with a panoramic view of the plaza directly in front of the theater.

"Château Wunder," Brunelle read the name of the cabaret, blazoned in red neon affixed to a building that otherwise would have passed as any other century-old government office building. "What does that mean?"

"Château. Wonder." Casey 'translated' with an exaggerated eye roll. "You really have no ear for languages, do you?"

"Does *château* mean the same thing in German as it does in English?" Brunelle ignored her jab.

Casey paused to stare at him for a moment. "It's French," she pointed out.

"Oh yeah," Brunelle nodded. "That makes sense."

"Does it?" Casey followed up.

"Not really," Brunelle admitted. "But if it makes sense to you, that's good enough for me. House of Wonder, here we come!"

"Château Wonder," Casey corrected. "House of Wonder would be *Wunderhaus*."

Brunelle cocked his head at her. "Are we really doing this?"

Casey sighed. "I guess not." She tugged his arm to start their gait again. "Let's go enjoy dinner and a show while we try to act inconspicuous asking questions about the murdered owner."

"In English," Brunelle added, a bit too cheerily.

Casey sighed again. "Sure," she acquiesced. "Why not?"

* * *

If the outside of Château Wunder had seemed retro on top of even more retro, the interior was future on top of infinite future. Outside had been red neon on gray stone. Inside was light upon more light, throbbing blue and purple, pulsating indigo and cyan. At the edges of the lobby were a dozen columns that looked like waterfalls of light. The walls behind the columns brightened and faded in a pleasing but unpredictable pattern. Even the floor glowed a cool pink, waves of light pulling Brunelle and Casey toward the theater entrance at the far end of the lobby.

Even the other patrons in the lobby seemed out of time. No tourists wearing their best t-shirts. Everyone wore some variation of evening wear, but the styles were European and eclectic, leaving the impression of another era, bygone or yet-to-come.

"*Karten, bitte,*" the man guarding the theater entrance demanded when they stepped up to him. "*Billets, s'il vous plaît.* Tickets, please."

Multiple languages, just like the song.

Casey presented her phone, and the ticket taker scanned the code on the screen, then waived them through. A few steps later they were inside the theater where the actual show would take place. The stage was at the far end of the room, a velvet curtain concealing whatever might lay beyond. Stretching back from the stage was a zigzag walkway, for the servers bringing food and drinks to the tables for two, three, and four guests. At the very front, right up against the stage, was the VIP section, bottles of champagne already on the tables. In the very back, right in front of the servers' station, was the standing section, offering a rail to set drinks on, but little more. Even that seemed luxurious somehow, with its combination of mahogany, steel, and red leather. Which was nice for Brunelle and Casey, because those were the only spots left when Casey went to buy tickets for a same day show.

"We have to stand way back here?" Brunelle complained after Casey led him straight ahead to the standing section, rather than down the winding path to leather seats and complimentary champagne.

Casey shrugged. "This is what was left." She squinted toward the distant stage. "But it's not like we came here for the show anyway."

Brunelle gave a small shrug. "I was more concerned with my knees giving out."

Casey grinned and patted him on the back. "You're not starting to feel your age, are you, lover?"

Brunelle stood up a bit straighter. "My age has nothing to do with it," he insisted. "I'm planning on drinking a lot, is all."

Casey laughed. "Then be glad about our tickets." She pointed behind them. "The bar is right there."

And so it was, right next to the servers' station and the coatroom. Not close to the stage, but definitely convenient. He nodded toward the bar. "Well, then let's get started, shall we? How do you say Manhattan in German?"

Casey cocked her head at him, then smiled. "'Man-hat-tan.' If you can remember that."

Brunelle nodded. "I can remember that. Now let's get two of those and settle in before we lose our prime spot at the center of the rail."

* * *

The show itself was very… German. Bold and beautiful, strange and disturbing, artistic and base. It was somehow erotic and repulsive at the same time, careening between the sensual and the absurd. The performers were a troupe of eight men and women, with bodies somehow both squat and athletic yet lithe and sexy, depending on what the number called for. Several bits involved trapeze. Another, hula hoops. Yet another, rubber balloons pulled through their noses in a way that was inexplicably but undeniably arousing. The performance was far more intoxicating than any of the several *Man-hat-tans* Brunelle ordered from the bar directly behind them.

"That was… exhilarating," Brunelle gasped as the house lights came up for intermission.

"Right?" Casey agreed, as the other patrons began heading for the restrooms and the staff swooped in to pick up empty plates and glasses. "No wonder this place is packed every night. Ferensz must have been the richest man in Berlin."

Brunelle shook his head. "So, why would a nobody like Mathias Ginkel murder him?"

Before Casey could reply with any hypothesis, the busboy leaning between them to grab Brunelle's empty Manhattan glasses stopped mid-slant. "Mathias Ginkel?" he asked. "You know Mathias?"

His English was good—a relief to Brunelle—but his accent was foreign. Not German. Italian, maybe?

"Uh, kind of," Brunelle answered. He glanced questioningly at Casey.

"Was he a friend of yours?" Casey jumped in.

The busboy shrugged, a dirty glass in each hand. "Yes, I suppose so. He and I work together. I know him."

"You work at Spa Balibai, too?" Brunelle asked

The busboy looked confused. "Spa? I do not work at a spa. I work here, at the cabaret theater."

"But Mathias worked at the Balibai Spa," Casey explained.

"I do not know anything about that," the young man said. "I only know that I work with Mathias here. He cleans the tables, just like me. Only," he paused, "he does not come to work for his last two shifts. He was supposed to work tonight, but again he does not come to work."

"That's because he was arrested," Brunelle said.

"Arrested?" the busboy asked. "I do not know this word. Stopped?" he guessed, likely based on a cognate from his own, yet to be determined, native language.

"Arrested," Casey repeated. "By the police."

"*Gefängnis*," Brunelle tried.

That seemed to do the trick.

"*Gefängnis*?!" the busboy exclaimed. His German was better than his English.

"*Mord*," Casey elaborated. "He was arrested for murder."

The busboy went slack. Brunelle expected him to drop the glasses in his hand, but somehow he managed to hold onto them.

Instead, after a moment, he managed to open his mouth wide enough to ask, "Whom did he kill?"

Brunelle and Casey looked at each other, then around at the House that Ferensz Built.

"Uh..." Brunelle started.

"That doesn't matter," Casey answered. "Do you think he's capable of killing someone?"

The busboy took a moment, then looked back at Casey. "I think we all are."

Brunelle had to nod at that. Wisdom from the mouths of busboys.

Casey changed tack. "Did he like working here? Do you? What is Mr. Ferensz like?"

That's when the busboy dropped the glasses. "Oh, no. Mr. Ferensz... he just died. They told us. He was shot. Oh my God. Mathias shot Mr. Ferensz?!"

Casey looked to Brunelle, who took a moment, then shrugged.

"Yes," Casey confirmed. "At least the police think so."

"Are you the police?" the busboy suddenly realized he had no idea who he was talking to. "Mathias and I, we do *Schwarzarbeit*. We have no choice. We need work. Mathias is very poor. I am from Romania and need work."

"What's shwoortz-whatever he said?" Brunelle asked Casey.

"*Schwarzarbeit*," Casey repeated. "It means getting paid under the table." She turned back to the busboy. "We're not the police," Casey assured, arguably correct since she was way out of her jurisdiction. "We're just a couple of American tourists."

"Then, how do you know all this?" the busboy asked. "Why are you asking me questions?"

"We were there the night Mr. Ferensz was shot," Brunelle admitted. "So, we've been following the case. That's all."

The busboy glanced nervously between them. The house lights flashed. The show was about to start up again.

"Was Mr. Ferensz a good boss?" Casey asked quickly as people began returning to their seats, and standing places.

The busboy frowned and took a step back. "Yes. Of course. I don't know. He was the boss. I tried to stay away from him. Mathias did too."

"Not far enough," Brunelle muttered.

"I must go now," the busboy said. He pointed toward the stage even as the lights began to dim in earnest. "The show."

Brunelle began to turn back toward the curtain, but Casey tugged his arm. "We need to go too," she whispered.

Brunelle offered a quizzical expression. "Where?"

"Backstage."

CHAPTER 12

"Backstage?" Brunelle whispered back at Casey.

She was pulling him through the crowd of the last people returning to their seats even as the curtain was beginning to rise. He resisted, his neck craning to see the stage, in part because he wanted to see the rest of the show, but mostly because he thought she was crazy.

"Are you crazy?" Brunelle hissed once they were stopped in the darkened hallway outside the doors to the theater. "Why would we do that? And how would we even know how to get there?"

"I'm a cop, remember?" Casey grinned. "You ever been to a crime scene?"

"Of course, I have," Brunelle answered. "I'm a prosecutor, remember?"

Casey chuckled in the darkness. "You've been to a crime scene after we cleaned it up. You've never walked into someplace not knowing who or what was waiting for you. You've never kicked in a door, gun drawn, hoping you see them before they see you. You don't know to always look left first if you're going to turn right. No, when you walk into a room, everybody stands up."

"That's the judge," Brunelle pointed out. "What's your point?"

"My point is," Casey explained, "when you were staring at all the pretty flashing lights in the lobby, I was scoping out the floor plan. I was checking for exits and entrances, guards and flunkies. I was making sure I knew where every door went and if anyone thought it was important enough to put somebody in front of it." She nodded behind him. "I found the entrance to backstage."

Brunelle turned around and squinted into the gloom. "Is there anyone in front of it?"

"Nope," Casey answered. Then, almost disappointedly, she added, "There's no one guarding any of the doors."

Brunelle thought for a moment. "Well, that's good. They probably aren't running a drug cartel out of the back of the theater."

"Although that would make for a good storyline," Casey observed.

Brunelle frowned a bit and shrugged. "Eh, cliché."

"Yeah," Casey agreed. Then she grabbed his arm again and spun him around. "Come on. If Mr. Ferensz wasn't running drugs out of this place, let's see what he was doing that might have led a lowly, paid-under-the-table busboy to murder him."

She led Brunelle behind the theater, down a long hallway, darkened lest a crack of light burst into the theater when a patron returned from the restroom. He let himself be pulled along by the hand, confident in Casey's reconnaissance and pleased regardless to be holding her hand.

The hallway curved around the back of the theater; Brunelle could hear music through the wall, and he wondered what amazing act the cast was performing to start Act II. His eyes were beginning to adjust to the darkness, and he could see the hallway end at a T intersection a few feet ahead. When they reached it, Casey pulled up short and peered at the wall directly in front of them.

There were two words Brunelle didn't understand, one short and one long, both written in red paint, and each had an arrow above it, pointing in opposite directions. Long word to the right, short word to the left.

"What does it say?" he whispered.

Casey nodded to their right. "Backstage is that way."

Brunelle took a step to his right, but Casey didn't follow. "Why aren't we moving?"

"Because the other way is the office," Casey answered. "I'm betting there's more incriminating evidence in the office than backstage."

"So, there was no plan for backstage specifically?" Brunelle complained. "I missed the second act because you just wanted to snoop around somewhere?"

Casey smiled at him, then popped a kiss on his cheek. "Yup. Now, come on." She tugged him to the left. "Let's hope there's no one in there while the show is going on."

Brunelle let himself be pulled farther into the darkness. "Yes," he muttered to himself. "Let's hope."

The journey to the office was a quick one. The darkened hallway led to a short staircase, mercifully illuminated from light escaping under the office door. Brunelle could tell it was the office because the door bore the same short word from the hallway. Also, Casey announced, "Here's the office."

She let go of Brunelle's hand and crept up the steps, pausing on each one to make sure it didn't squeak. When she reached the top, she tried the door handle. It opened with an audible, but not particularly loud, click.

"We're in," Casey whispered.

Brunelle managed a half-smile. "But are we alone?" he voiced what he thought was the more pressing question.

As it turned out, yes, they were alone. The office was empty, despite the lights being on. The computer on the desk was also on, its screen not yet timed out to black. The room had the definite feel of its occupant only taking a quick bathroom break. Then again, Brunelle hadn't seen any bathrooms on their way there, and they hadn't passed anyone either, so maybe the trip all the way to the lobby and back wouldn't be that quick after all.

"We should hurry," he counseled anyway.

Casey seemed to agree as she was already pulling open desk drawers with one hand and flipping through papers with the other.

The office was smallish, with no real view. It was an old building, so the windows were small and spaced apart. The only thing visible past the curtains on either side was a series of similar windows from the building right next door. Otherwise, there was only the desk Casey was rummaging through, a tall wooden file cabinet, two wooden guest chairs that looked extremely uncomfortable, and a short leather couch placed against the aforementioned windows. A half-filled teacup and saucer sat on the table next to the couch.

"We really should get going," Brunelle whispered to Casey. "I'm one hundred percent sure this is trespassing, even under German law."

"We got lost," Casey offered. "I'm looking for directions back to our seats."

"Our standing places," Brunelle corrected. "And there's

no way I'm going with that story. I'm just glad I know I don't have to answer any police questions here either. One thing I can thank Mathias Ginkel for."

The next few minutes passed like hours for Brunelle. Each click of the old-fashioned clock on the wall felt like a leaden eternity as Casey continued her examination of the books and papers she found, first in the desk and then the file cabinet. Finally, she pushed the last of the file drawers closed and turned to look at Brunelle, fists on her hips and a puzzled frown on her lips.

"Nothing," she announced, not at all in a whisper.

"Nothing?" Brunelle repeated. "Like, no information about the business, or the employees, or what?"

"Worse," Casey said. "There is plenty of information, and all of it looks perfectly legit. Well, except paying a few of the employees under the table. That's between them and the German tax collectors. But from everything I saw, it's a competently run, successful business."

"Well, that's disappointing," Brunelle replied.

"Right?" Casey agreed. "They had a transition plan in place, and they executed the plan. The business is incorporated and although Ferensz was the majority stockholder, there were others, and the board smartly kept on the long-time theater manager for continuity of operations. Some guy named Hans-Peter Oberflacher. The first thing he did was up their security after an employee murdered the boss."

"Smart," Brunelle observed.

"Definitely. But also boring," Casey grumbled. "I was hoping for some evidence of a crime."

"Well, we are trespassing," Brunelle pointed out again, "so at least there's that."

As if to drive Brunelle's point home, a faint whistling became audible from the hallway. It was quickly getting louder as its owner—likely the theater manager who had been drinking tea and working on his computer before taking a bathroom break—approached the office door. Brunelle scanned the room for another door, but Casey had done that when they first entered, he supposed, because she was already pulling up the sash on one of the windows.

"Come on!" she whisper-yelled, summoning him over with a flail of her hand. "Fire escape!"

Brunelle wanted to hesitate—maybe they could talk their way out of it?—but his instincts took over and he scrambled out the window behind Casey onto a frighteningly narrow and rickety iron fire escape. In fact, it was little more than one long ladder to the ground, with a small shelf-like landing at each floor. Casey slid down, hands grasping the iron rails on either side, her feet avoiding the delay of actually stepping on each individual rung. Brunelle followed suit, but slower, actually using the ladder as a ladder, rather than a fireman's pole.

Casey landed first on the alley behind the theater. Brunelle hit the pavement a few seconds later, one of his feet landing in a puddle left over from the last time the abutting businesses had sprayed down the alleyway. There were three very large men loitering outside the backstage door, wearing the tuxedo-like uniforms of ushers, smoking cigarettes, and turning their heads when Brunelle's foot made its splash.

All three of their heads looked at Casey and Brunelle, then up the fire escape to the theater office, then back down at Casey and Brunelle. Then all three of them flicked their cigarettes aside and started walking toward the fallen Americans.

Casey yanked at Brunelle's arm one last time. "Run!"

CHAPTER 13

Running in high heels was difficult but not impossible. Brunelle had done it once himself. But Casey made it look like an Olympic sport and she was the reigning gold medalist. Brunelle sprinted after her even as the Three Stooges dropped into a full run as well, yelling after them in words Brunelle didn't understand but could guess from context.

Casey ducked down the first side alley that presented itself. It was all Brunelle could do not to slip on the smooth asphalt as he tried to cut sharply in his dress shoes. He put out an arm to bounce off the brick wall of the building he was sliding into and righted himself to chase after Casey who was already farther ahead than he would have expected. Under different circumstances, his manhood might have felt slighted, but he had three much larger manhoods bearing down on him, so he lowered his head and ran as fast as he could after the retreating form of his amazingly fast girlfriend.

Casey cut down another side alley. Brunelle followed, barely in time to see her do it again up ahead. The shouts from the Germans were getting louder. Brunelle turned back to steal a look as he made the next turn and they were already closer to him than he was to Casey. One more side alley and Casey had disappeared completely from view. He was on his own. But she was safe.

Easy decision.

Brunelle pulled up short, and turned to face his pursuers, fists raised, chest heaving, and legs burning. Maybe he could talk his way out of it. If they spoke English.

The three men stumbled to a stop as well, surprised to find Brunelle squared up at them as they turned the corner. Surprised, but amused. Laughter sounded the same in every language. So did the cracking of knuckles.

Brunelle wasn't a particularly small man, and he probably had an individual size advantage over two of the three of them, but the third one was several inches and a couple dozen pounds bigger than him. Plus, there were three of them and Brunelle doubted they were planning on taking numbers. The largest of them stepped forward. He had a fat head with hair cropped almost to the skin and too much pink around his eyes and mouth.

"I'm sure we can work this out," Brunelle tried, taking a step back, to gain a few inches distance and surer footing. "You look like reasonable men."

It's not a lie if the other person doesn't understand you anyway.

The Big Guy laughed, his thick lips parting into a stubby-toothed grin. He shouted something back toward his compatriots, who added their laughter to his. It wasn't going well. Brunelle pushed his weight onto that back foot.

Big Guy yelled something more, this time at Brunelle, and with more scowl than smile. It had a question mark at the end, but Brunelle didn't imagine his answer would have mattered anyway. He readied himself to duck under the first swing and throw a punch back into Big Guy's stomach, hopefully surprising him and knocking the wind out of him. That might give Brunelle a chance to escape if Big Guy's friends decided to attend to their comrade rather than pursue Brunelle as he attempted again to escape.

Big Guy was faster than he looked. And left-handed, apparently. That first punch landed on Brunelle's temple before he knew it was coming. Brunelle crumpled to the ground. He would have been disappointed that he didn't even get a shot in if he could have assembled any thoughts beyond '*Ouch*' and '*Uh-oh*'.

He hit the pavement hard, his left shoulder the only thing preventing his head from hitting the pavement directly. He had a vague sense of relief for that. He'd prosecuted manslaughter cases where one punch sent someone to the ground skull first, leading to death by brain bleed. He felt less fortunate when he managed to focus his eyes enough to identify the large boot placed directly in front of his face. He looked up at Big Guy, which only confirmed the German was even pinker and fattier and uglier from that angle. Brunelle put one arm in front of his face and used the other to start pushing himself off the pavement. He wasn't going down without a fight. Well, not a second time anyway.

Big Guy seemed glad for it and gave Brunelle the time and space to stand up again. No sport in kicking a man when he was down. Apparently, Big Guy was all about sportsmanship.

Brunelle wasn't. He feigned a weak punch then kicked Big Guy as hard as he could right between the legs.

It had the desired effect. Well, one of its effects was desired. Big Guy let out a wail and dropped to one knee, grasping at his crotch. The other effects were less desirable. Big Guy was more angry than actually injured; that stupid grin of his was gone. And his two friends were done waiting their turns.

Brunelle was about to get his ass kicked. That fatal brain bleed was a definite possibility.

Then came the gunshot.

Brunelle instinctively ducked. He didn't think they were armed. They ducked too. They weren't armed.

But Junior Inspector Dieter Vorsburg was.

"Hey!" Dieter shouted as he stepped out of the shadows.

Actually, he yelled several more words, but Brunelle could only understand that first one. The others understood the rest of them though, or at least they understood the warning shot Dieter had fired. There was a weak attempt at explanation, with half-gestures toward Brunelle and a justifying tone to their response, but they stepped back, then forewent any further argument in favor of running away.

Brunelle dropped to one knee himself. His head was still spinning, partly from the blow and partly from all the adrenaline his body had dumped into his bloodstream. His fingers tingled and his ears were still ringing from the gunshot. "Dieter? How? How did you--? Why are you even here?"

Dieter holstered his gun and laughed. "I have more than our one case, Davey." He put an arm under Brunelle's and helped him back to his feet. "You're just lucky I was nearby when I heard those criminals laughing and shouting."

Brunelle couldn't deny that. He nodded, which hurt. "Thanks," he said, cradling his head in his hands. "I owe you."

Casey came running up to them at that point, from the same direction she had disappeared into. "Dave!" she shouted. "Oh my God, Dave, are you okay?"

"Dave?" Dieter asked.

"Davey," Brunelle managed to stick with the lie despite the circumstances.

"Shut up," Casey admonished him. She pulled Brunelle's hands from his head to inspect him for injuries. "I heard the gunshot. What happened?"

"Dieter saved my life," Brunelle gestured toward the German policeman. Then he remembered at least some of his male bravado. "I mean, you should see the other guy."

Casey touched the growing bump on his temple ever so slightly. Brunelle recoiled. "Did you even get a punch in?"

"I got a kick in," Brunelle defended. "We both went down once. Then the cavalry arrived."

"Who were they?' Dieter asked. "Why did they attack you?"

Brunelle winced, only partly from the lingering pain, and looked to Casey for direction.

"Uh…" she started. "No idea. We have no idea."

"Maybe they just didn't like Americans," Brunelle suggested.

Dieter frowned. "They were dressed like ushers. And you two are dressed for the theater. Did something happen at the cabaret? That was your plan for the evening, no?"

"Yes," Brunelle admitted. "But if they were from the theater, I don't know. They saw us outside and started chasing us."

"Probably just a mugging," Casey suggested.

"Mugging?" Dieter questioned.

"Uh, *Straßenraub*," Casey translated.

"I know what it means," Dieter replied. "I am simply not accustomed to seeing muggers wearing tuxedos."

"They were more like tuxedo-inspired formal wear," Brunelle observed. "Not actual tuxedos per se."

Dieter took a moment, then asked, "Are you okay, Dave?"

"Davey," Brunelle insisted again. He took advantage of the momentary change in topic, hoping to make it more permanent. "And maybe not." He put a hand back to where he'd been punched. "I should probably get back to the hotel."

"Perhaps you should go to the hospital?" Dieter suggested. "I can drive you."

"No, no," Brunelle waved the suggestion away. "I can take a punch. And thanks to you, I only had to take the one."

"Yes, thank you," Casey said, touching Dieter's arm. "I can take care of him from here."

"Are you sure you don't want a ride home?" Dieter asked. "My car is right around the corner."

More time with Dieter meant more questions from Dieter. Brunelle and Casey both understood that.

"No," Brunelle insisted. "Just walk us to the main street, then we'll make our way back to the hotel. I could use some fresh air. I don't think we'll see those goons again."

Casey nodded in agreement as she steered Brunelle toward the main road. "Yeah, we got this. I promise."

Dieter frowned, but relented. "Okay. But let's meet again tomorrow and you can tell me whatever it is you're hiding from me now."

CHAPTER 14

The next morning, Brunelle's head definitely hurt. A dull throb behind his eye and over his ear. But it was his shoulder that was really painful. Everything in Europe seemed a little bit smaller, and the bed was no exception. It was big enough for two people, but it wasn't big enough for one of them to roll over without waking the other one up. So, Brunelle had spent the entire night in one position, and the shoulder that had hit the pavement felt like it had a spike driven through it.

He forced himself into a sitting position with an almost embarrassingly loud groan. He wasn't sure if he was feeling his age exactly, but he was feeling somebody's age, and that person needed to get more exercise and eat better.

"You okay?" Casey propped herself up on her own uninjured arm and touched his back.

"Yeah," Brunelle answered. He tried to rotate his shoulder but stopped at the immediate shock of pain that shot up his neck into the back of his skull. "Just a little sore still."

"You should see the other guy, I hear," Casey joked.

That brought a smile to Brunelle's face. "I hope he's as

sore where I hit him as I am where I hit the ground."

Casey threw off the covers and stood up. "I'll see if we have any ice in the mini-fridge."

Brunelle didn't protest, although he doubted the ice would do much good. He just needed to move it around a little. He stood up and followed her into the kitchenette. "Who were those guys anyway?" he asked from the doorframe.

"They're probably thinking the same thing about us," Casey opined, as she crouched in front of the half-sized refrigerator. She pulled out a chilled mini-bottle of champagne. "We have this," she offered.

Brunelle tried to shrug in agreement, but that sent the same bolt of pain into the base of his skull. "Sure," he managed to say after a moment. He took it from her and placed it where his shoulder met his neck. "Thanks."

"They already know more about us than we do about them," Casey continued. "White man, Black woman, American tourists, sneaking out of the theater office. It's a good thing they ran from Dieter instead of making a trespassing report."

"They might not know we're Americans," Brunelle suggested.

"You tried to talk your way out of it, right?" Casey knew.

Brunelle grinned. "Well, yeah," he admitted. "Of course, I did."

"Of course, you did." Casey nodded. "So, again, they know a lot more about us than we do about them."

"We know they work there," Brunelle offered. "I mean, probably. I guess they could have been dressed up to go see the show, instead of working there."

Casey raised a hand to her chin. "Maybe, but they were out back, smoking by the backstage entrance. I think we can conclude they were employees. But we're going to need more time to figure out what's going on."

"Because there's no way we're telling Dieter what really happened, right?" Brunelle asked.

"Oh, no way in hell," Casey confirmed. "We're on our own now."

Brunelle set the bottle of champagne on the counter. "I'll call the airline to push back our return flight."

"I'll call the front desk to book us another week," Casey followed up.

"And then are we going where I think we're going?" Brunelle asked.

Casey smiled and nodded. "Yep."

"Good." Brunelle rubbed his neck. "Maybe I can grab a massage while we're there."

CHAPTER 15

Spa Balibai. The words stood above the main entrance, painted to resemble the artwork and alphabets of Southeast Asia. Brunelle hadn't noticed that before, but he was looking at everything with new eyes. Not the eyes of an American tourist, or of a lovesick schoolboy on a date with a pretty girl, but the eyes of a homicide prosecutor, of the person responsible not necessarily for solving the case but for proving to twelve strangers there was no reasonable doubt about that solution.

He'd been to plenty of crime scenes before, always with a dual role. The first was to ensure the cops didn't make some small mistake that might result in evidence being overlooked or worse, collected but then suppressed at trial. The second was simply to soak up the place, to understand it in three dimensions and five senses so he could convey all that to those same twelve people who hadn't been there when the evidence was fresh. Who, even if they visited the scene, would be visiting a scene that had been cleaned up and papered over, with the very intent of concealing anything bad had ever happened there.

Exactly like the scene they were walking into right then,

Brunelle considered with a slight frown.

Spa Balibai was a business, and murder was bad for business—unless you were in Brunelle's and Casey's business. So, Brunelle knew as they passed under that sign and through the front doors, the owners had done everything in their power to wash away any evidence that one of their employees had murdered one of their guests and left his body in one of the pools, bobbing like a Halloween apple.

Casey looked sideways at him. "What are you thinking?"

Brunelle snapped back to his surroundings. "What? Why?"

"You have a stupid grin on your face," Casey informed him. "Don't start talking about Halloween apples or anything dumb like that."

Brunelle tried to laugh it off. "Halloween what? No, I don't know what you're talking about. All good. Everything is good."

They were approaching the reception desk.

"You still want that massage?" Casey asked.

Brunelle's attention returned to his neck, which was still pretty sore actually. "Um, sure?" He did, but he had been joking. It didn't seem like the most efficient use of time.

"Good," Casey answered. "You see if the masseuse knows anything about our killer or our victim. I'll snoop around the pool areas and see if the attendants saw anything."

Brunelle considered for a moment. "What do I do if she doesn't speak English?"

Casey smiled. "Just enjoy your massage."

Brunelle nodded. He could do that.

* * *

In the event, the person did speak English, and he was a

masseur not a masseuse.

Brunelle had never gotten a massage from a man before, let alone a European man.

"*Guten Tag.* Good afternoon," the man said as Brunelle entered the massage room, wearing only the thin robe he'd pulled on while discarding his street clothes in a locker in the changing room. He was giving Brunelle the choice: German or English. Not much of a choice. As it turned out.

"Uh, good afternoon," Brunelle returned. "Hi."

The masseur was tall, dark, and handsome. Really. He was probably 6'6", with sinewy muscles under olive skin. He had thick black hair and a neatly trimmed beard. "Take off your robe, please," he instructed in accented English, "and lay on the table."

Under different circumstances, Brunelle imagined some of the other patrons would have enjoyed hearing that from someone like the masseur. It made Brunelle suddenly very aware that he was naked, or about to be. He hung his robe on the hook that seemed ridiculously far away from the massage table, then scurried to lay face down in a futile attempt to somehow conceal his nudity.

"I am Nikos," the masseur offered his name.

Brunelle took a moment before realizing he probably ought to offer his own. "Um, Dave. I'm Dave. Or Davey," he quipped nervously, then regretted it. "No, Dave. Well, David. But yeah, just Dave."

Why was he so nervous? Wasn't there something else he was supposed to be doing?

Nikos loudly squirted some oil on his hands and even more loudly rubbed his hands together, before slapping them down on Brunelle's shoulders. "Where does it hurt, David?"

Right fucking there, Brunelle thought as the pain shot from Nikos's iron grip up into the back of his head and halfway down his back.

"Uh, actually," Brunelle finally gasped. "My left shoulder. It hurts. Right there. Where you're grabbing."

Nikos relaxed his grip. "You have injured your shoulder?"

"Yes," Brunelle exhaled through gritted teeth.

"How did you injure it?" Nikos inquired.

"Long story," Brunelle said. "You should see the other guy."

Nikos shook his head. "What other guy? I do not understand."

"It's a joke," Brunelle explained. "Never mind. I fell and landed on it, hard."

"Ah," Nikos responded. He lifted his hands from Brunelle's lats and glided a skilled finger to the edge of Brunelle's left shoulder. He pressed the finger down ever so slightly. "Here?"

Brunelle shook his head slightly. "No, a little higher, I think?"

The finger traced upward then pressed in again. Brunelle winced. "Yeah," he inhaled. "That's it."

Nikos pulled his finger away for a moment, then grabbed Brunelle's shoulder a bit more vigorously than Brunelle would have thought warranted under the circumstances. "This may hurt," Nikos warned.

Brunelle recoiled at the warning, propping himself up and pulling his shoulder out of Nikos's strong hands. "That's okay. I'm not looking to get hurt more."

Nikos laughed, then put a reassuring palm on Brunelle's

back. "Relax, David." He pressed down on Brunelle's back, firmly, and Brunelle let himself return to the massage table. "I have many years of experience. Trust me."

Brunelle wasn't sure he actually trusted Nikos, but he finally remembered the assignment Casey had given him.

"Many years of experience, huh?" Brunelle asked as Nikos lifted his left arm out straight, then stuck a finger into his armpit. "Um, ouch."

"Yes," Nikos answered, although Brunelle wasn't sure it was in response to his question or his expression of pain.

Nikos probed deeper with his finger even as he raised Brunelle's arm at a series of increasingly awkward angles.

"Uh, so—*oof*—have all of those years been here?" Brunelle pressed on with his inquiries despite the discomfort in his shoulder. "At Spa Balibai?"

Nikos relaxed his grip on Brunelle's arm and returned it to his side. "No, not all." He placed both his large hands over Brunelle's shoulder blade and began probing at the edges of the bone. "I have worked here for more than two years now."

"Two years? Wow," Brunelle got out before another "Ouch." Then, "So, I suppose you get to—*ow*—know everyone after a while, huh?"

"Know everyone?" Nikos repeated.

"Right, like, the other massage therapists," Brunelle grunted. Whatever Nikos was doing it was really starting to hurt. "Uh, the people at the front desk. Ouch. Um, the towel boys, maybe?"

Nikos stopped driving his fingers into Brunelle's skeleton. "The towel boys?" he questioned.

"Um, yeah." Brunelle took a deep breath again at the cessation of pain. "The young men who clean up the towels from the locker room and probably the massage rooms, too, I would guess."

"You are interested in having a towel boy," Nikos crossed his arms, "go to a massage room with you?"

Brunelle leaned up onto his good arm. "Um, no," he assured Nikos. "That's not what I meant. I'm just wondering... that is... I mean..."

He sighed. He was used to asking questions in a courtroom, fully clothed, where the witness had to answer, and he controlled the interview. He'd never had a witness misinterpret his questions as soliciting underage sex.

"Look," he decided to cut to the chase. "My girlfriend and I were here the night that man, Viktor Ferensz, was murdered. We found out later an employee named Mathias Ginkel was arrested for the crime. Did you know either of them?"

Nikos stepped back and took a long moment to appraise the naked man on his massage table. Finally, he crossed his arms and asked the obvious question. "Who are you?"

Oh, right, Brunelle thought. *That.*

"Um, just a curious tourist," Brunelle answered. Not entirely untrue. It wasn't like he had any real standing in the official investigation.

"You are curious about towel boys," Nikos asked, arms still crossed and one eyebrow raised, "and Mathias Ginkel and Viktor Ferensz. It sounds to me like you already know everything you need to know."

"Wait." Brunelle started to push himself into a seated position, then decided against exposing his genitals at that exact moment. "You mean, Ferensz and Ginkel were, uh...?" He resisted the urge to make a sex gesture with his fingers. He hoped his tone and undoubtedly stupid expression were getting the point across.

"I mean," Nikos answered, finally uncrossing his arms but his expression not becoming any less stern, "your massage is done. You may put your robe back on. I am leaving now."

"Damn." Brunelle flopped back down on the massage table, which only served to send another shock of pain through his shoulder and neck. Nikos left him alone in the room and he let out a long sigh. "That went well."

* * *

"What did you find out?" Casey asked him when she rendezvoused with him at the bar some 45 minutes later.

"I found out," he began, as Casey pulled out the stool next to him and sat down, "that soliciting sex with towel boys is frowned upon here, although it is perhaps not without precedent."

Casey took a moment to stare at him, eyebrows knitted together. "What the hell kind of massage did you order?"

Brunelle laughed a little, which made his neck twinge again. "A very short one," he answered. "It ended right after I asked about Ginkel and Ferensz."

"I'm not surprised," Casey answered. "So, you came out of the gate with the whole sex with towel boys thing? Bold."

"No," Brunelle insisted, leaning an elbow on the bar to take some pressure off his shoulder. "There was a language barrier, I think, and so the massage guy kind of misunderstood me."

"Oh, sure, that makes sense." Casey rolled her eyes. "'Where does it hurt?' 'I'd like to fuck a towel boy.' Happens all the time."

Brunelle frowned at her. "Are you done?"

Casey put a thoughtful hand to her chin. "Do I have to be?

I mean, I feel like this is one I can circle back to a few times."

Brunelle nodded, then gestured for the bartender. "Order me something strong," he told Casey. "Then you can make one more joke and tell me what you found out."

Casey turned to the approaching bartender and ordered two of something, then turned back to Brunelle. "I ordered you a Drunken Towel Boy with a lemon twist."

"Why does he have to be drunk?" Brunelle protested.

"Really?" Casey laughed. "That's why you're upset? You want to make sure the towel boy is sober?"

Brunelle shrugged. "I mean, I don't want him to have to be drunk."

Casey leaned forward and kissed him on the cheek. "Don't worry, Davey. Any towel boy would be lucky to have to blow you for twenty bucks."

"Again," Brunelle protested, "'have to'?"

Casey shook her head. "You know what? I am done after all. Well done."

"Thanks." Brunelle offered a satisfied grin. "Now, what did you find out?"

"More than I expected, actually," Casey responded. "And maybe connected to what you found out."

Brunelle cocked his head at her. "What do you mean?"

"I've been chatting up any employee I could find, Casey explained. "You know, the typical, 'Oh, my gosh, I can't believe what happened' stuff, except in German."

"Of course," Brunelle encouraged, even as the bartender brought what appeared to be some sort of sangria concoction. "Go on."

"Well, most of them weren't sure if they should talk to me at first," Casey continued, "but there's always that one person who can't shut up about it. In this case, her name was Helga."

"Really? Helga?" Brunelle was surprised. "Okay. So, what did Helga have to say? In German, of course."

"Of course," Casey agreed. "Well, Helga seems to know everyone's business and is proud of it too. She told me that Ginkel had only been working here for a short time, but he immediately caught the eye of Ferensz, who's been a customer of this place since it opened like four years ago."

"Caught the eye?" Brunelle repeated. "As in...?" That time he went ahead and did the hand gesture for sex.

But Casey put her hand to her chin again. "That's what Helga guessed, but she wasn't sure. She said on one of the first days Ginkel was working, Ferensz pulled her aside and asked who he was. She figured it was sexual because it was kind of weird how he did it. But she never actually saw them doing anything. No one ever caught them in the sauna or anything like that."

"So, maybe he had some other interest in Ginkel," Brunelle surmised.

"Or maybe he knew Ginkel from somewhere else," Casey suggested, "but didn't know his name."

"Like the cabaret," Brunelle realized.

"Exactly."

"How long ago was that?" Brunelle followed up.

"About three months." Casey answered. "Helga wasn't exactly sure, but everyone I talked to thought Ginkel had started about three, maybe four months ago."

Brunelle nodded and took a long drink of his sangria. "Good work, detective," he said. "Now, let's book a couple's massage. My neck is still killing me."

"Should we try to get the same guy who walked out on

you?" Casey laughed.

"Why not?" Brunelle smiled. He gestured at his lovely girlfriend. "I'd like him to see I can do a lot better than some random towel boy."

CHAPTER 16

Brunelle knew they were going to see Dieter again. He just didn't expect it to be as soon as they walked out of Spa Balibai.

"Hello, you two!" Dieter called out from his spot leaning against a light post at the end of the walk from the spa to the street. "You aren't trying to avoid me, are you? Or perhaps you are simply conducting your own investigation, eh?"

Brunelle was stunned for a moment. It was both of those things, obviously, and they all knew it. But Casey was quicker on her feet. Then again, she hadn't been in a fight the previous night.

"Dieter!" she shouted back. She raised her arms toward him and quickened her gait. "I'm so glad you're here. We have some new information."

Brunelle may have been slower, but he was also feeling a little more thorough. "What are you doing here anyway?" he asked as he closed the gap between himself and the others. "You're not here for a massage, are you?"

Dieter laughed. "Not any more than you are," he grinned. "I have my contacts and my sources. When people start asking questions about a murder investigation, I hear about it. When those people are a Black and white American couple, well, I know exactly who is asking the questions."

Brunelle frowned and glanced at Casey, who returned the expression. They did kind of stick out.

"Do not worry," Dieter continued. "I am not a proud man. If you can help the case against Mathias Ginkel, then I can only be happy about that. What did you learn?"

Brunelle was also happy to talk about what they'd just learned. It avoided the topic of what the hell they were doing in that alley behind Château Wunder last night. He didn't need to look at Casey to know she was thinking the same thing.

"Ginkel and Ferensz did know each other," Casey answered.

"And maybe more," Brunelle added, again with that hand gesture.

Dieter's eyebrow raised. "Really? That is surprising. I did not know how they knew each other. Or that perhaps…" He repeated Brunelle's hand gesture. Apparently, it spanned language barriers.

Casey rolled her eyes. "That is speculative at best, and can we stop having hand sex, please? Let's pretend we're adults."

Dieter nodded. "I can do that. So, they knew each other? That is interesting. It may perhaps help us uncover a motive."

"So, you don't have any other motive yet?" Casey asked.

"Young, poor man shoots old, rich man." Dieter shrugged. "Perhaps he was jealous. I don't know."

"Is motive an element of murder in Germany?" Brunelle inquired.

"Intent, yes, but not motive," Dieter responded. "But it can be hard to prove intent if you don't know the motive."

Brunelle nodded. "I've encountered the same problem."

"So, class jealousy?" Casey repeated. "That seems weak. Most people aren't willing to kill someone over that."

"I agree," Dieter replied. "That is why I believe this new theory," he repeated the sex gesture very quickly, with his hands held low, "may be more likely. I will look into it. Thank you. You two would make good detectives."

"I am a good detective." Casey crossed her arms. "In fact, I'm a good enough detective to know you didn't come here to ask us why we were asking about Ginkel and Ferensz."

Dieter took a moment before replying, like a child caught with the lid to the cookie jar in his hand, but not quite removed yet. A respectful smile unfurled across his lips. "Yes, you are a good detective, Casey Emory. I had almost forgotten that."

Brunelle appreciated the compliment to his girlfriend, but felt his gut clench at the prospect of the conversation turning to what they were doing in that back alley the previous night. Brunelle and Casey may not have seen who entered the theater office as they were scrambling out onto the fire escape, but that didn't mean whoever it was didn't see them.

But Dieter had other plans. "Sabine wants to speak with you." He pointed at Brunelle. "Specifically, she wants to speak with Davey."

Brunelle turned to Casey. "Is that getting old yet?"

Casey shook her head. "No, not yet." She looked to Dieter. "Just Davey? Like, was I specifically excluded?"

"I think so," Dieter answered. "She said 'lawyer to lawyer'. Well, actually she said, '*Anwältin zu Anwalt*', which translates as 'woman-lawyer to man-lawyer', but I don't think the gender mattered."

Brunelle frowned. He wasn't so sure.

CHAPTER 17

"You wanted to see me?" Brunelle started the conversation with Sabine Ehrenwald.

He and Casey had parted ways with Dieter as quickly as possible, somehow managing to avoid discussing the previous evening's events. Then they swung by the hotel so Brunelle could put on something more professional than the outfit he'd worn for a morning at the spa. Brunelle wasn't sure that was the way to play it, but Casey insisted. 'I think she likes you actually,' Casey had said. 'Use that.'

Brunelle had no desire at all to use anything of the sort. The last thing he needed on his romantic, albeit murder-filled, getaway with his still fairly new girlfriend was some sort of romantic entanglement with another woman. Especially a tall, starkly beautiful woman with chiseled features and penetrating eyes. All accentuated by the tight, perfectly tailored suit she was wearing when she came out to the lobby to greet Brunelle.

She frowned at him. "Ah, yes. I almost forgot I would have to speak English with you." She sighed, then hooked a finger at him and commanded, "Come with me."

Brunelle sighed too, but more because he already felt underdressed and outmatched. Casey wanted him to pump Sabine for information about Ginkel and Ferensz. But he was pretty sure he was the one who was about to get pumped.

"Sit down," Sabine directed when they reached her office. She was again wearing a sleeveless shell, black satin, and the way she pointed at the chair caused the sinews on the inside of her arm to pop. It was a good look on her.

"Yes, ma'am," Brunelle said before he could stop himself. He took a moment, then lowered himself into the chair in a way he hoped appeared not completely submissive.

Sabine didn't sit down in the large leather office chair on the other side of her desk. Instead, she sat down on the edge of her desk, directly in front of Brunelle and crossed her legs. She had very nice, very long legs. Her tight black skirt expertly covered everything else from view. His view. He forced himself to raise his eyes to hers. Her radiant blue eyes.

"Do you know why you are here, Mr. Brunelle?"

Brunelle could barely remember his own name, so, "No, ma'am, I don't."

He really needed to stop with the 'ma'am's.

"You are here, Mr. Brunelle," she leaned forward exposing very little, but precisely the right amount of skin on her chest, "you are here, *Davey*, because I need you."

Brunelle blinked at her. She didn't blink back. Those shimmering azure pools were unrelenting. "Y—You need me?" he stammered back. "For what?"

Brunelle knew he had a weakness for women who showed any sort of romantic or sexual interest in him. It had gotten him into trouble more than once in his life. He also knew that Sabine had absolutely, positively no real romantic or sexual interest in him. She was playing him. And yet, he was just glad he'd managed not to say 'ma'am' again.

Sabine smiled at him. It was a small smile, really only on the corners of her mouth. It was cold, calculating even, but it was also genuine somehow, even if only to her own purposes. The smile reached her eyes; they sparkled.

"I need you," she leaned in a little bit more, "to tell me the truth."

Brunelle nodded. He could do that. He just hoped she didn't ask what he was thinking right then. "Of course."

Her smile broadened, exposing impossibly white teeth—fangs almost. His neck felt suddenly exposed, too, but in a good way.

"Good," she almost purred. Then, without warning, she stood up sharply and marched around to the other side of her desk. She pulled a file from atop her file cabinet and slammed it down in front of Brunelle. "Do you think I can win this case?"

Brunelle involuntarily gave his head a sharp shake, as if waking from a dream—or fantasy, anyway. "What? Which case? This case? *The* case? The Ginkel case?"

"Yes, of course, the Ginkel case," Sabine practically spat. Still, an alluring spit, somehow. "Or are you involved in other murder cases in my city that I do not know about?"

"No, no, of course not." Brunelle raised his hands in protest. "And I'm not sure how involved I am, really…"

Did she know about their Adventures in Burglary from the night before?

"You are a witness," Sabine reminded him, "and my detective is allowing your," she hesitated as she chose her next word, "companion to assist with the ongoing investigation. I would say that makes you quite involved."

Brunelle shrugged slightly, "Well, I mean—"

"But that is not why I want your opinion," Sabine cut him off. "I want your opinion as a lawyer, as a state's lawyer."

"Prosecutor," Brunelle corrected. "We say prosecutor, not state's lawyer. At least where I'm from. I mean, maybe in some other states. Actually, I kind of prefer Assistant D.A. 'D.A.' is short for 'district attorney', but I'm not *the* District Attorney. That's an elected position. So, I'm not the D.A., I'm an assistant D.A. But not state's lawyer. And prosecutor is fine, too. Whatever. Really."

Sabine crossed her arms. She was still standing, and her smile had been wholly replaced with a glower. "Are you finished?"

Brunelle nodded. "Yes, ma'am."

"Good." She finally sat down. "This is a difficult case, with an important victim and an uncertain motive. I expect to win. I always expect to win. But the reason I always expect to win is because I do everything possible to win. I have been presented with a resource in you, Mr. Brunelle, and I intend to exploit that resource."

Brunelle raised a hesitant finger. "You might want to say 'use' that resource. 'Exploit' has a negative connotation. Like you intend to take what you want, then discard it like an empty husk."

Sabine stared at him for a moment, still unblinking. "Yes."

Brunelle wasn't sure what she was agreeing with, changing her phrasing or that she intended to exploit him and discard him like so much trash. He didn't get a chance to clarify.

"You said you prosecute murder cases, yes?" she asked.

"Yes," Brunelle confirmed. "That's pretty much all I do."

"Good." She tapped the top of the file. "These are all of

the narrative reports written by every officer involved in the investigation. You will read them. Then you will tell me where my case is weak and where it is strong. Then I will fix what is weak."

Brunelle frowned at the file. "That's in German, right? I can't read that."

Sabine rolled her eyes. "Then have your," again a pause, "companion translate it for you. Put her to some use for you."

Brunelle's eyebrows raised. He wasn't sure he would be telling Casey about that particular comment when he debriefed her on the meeting. "That's not really—" he started to protest.

"Oh, I am certain she will enjoy the opportunity to exhibit her skills for you," Sabine raised her voice a little. It was startling, and made Brunelle want to blurt out 'ma'am' again. "You have one day," Sabine continued. "You will tell me your thoughts tomorrow."

It was an easy decision. He was being given access to the full prosecution file. If he had some ideas, great. If not, what was the harm? "Tomorrow," he confirmed.

"Tomorrow," Sabine repeated. She stood up. "Over dinner."

"Dinner?" Brunelle almost choked.

"Nineteen o'clock," Sabine continued. "Seven in the evening, you Americans say, yes? The 'Edelstein' restaurant on Alexanderplatz. Bring the file. Do not be late."

Brunelle stood up, a bit dazed, and slowly pulled the file off Sabine's desk. He wasn't sure what had just happened, but he knew exactly what to say.

"Yes, ma'am."

CHAPTER 18

"That's fantastic!" Casey enthused when Brunelle told her what had happened at Sabine's office.

"It's fantastic I'm having dinner with another woman?" Brunelle queried.

Casey waved that notion away. "I don't care about that."

Brunelle was a bit hurt. "You could care a little," he suggested.

But Casey just laughed. "Whatever, Davey. She's sweet on you? Great. Use that." She patted the case file Brunelle had brought home to her. "Hell, you already used it. See what else you can get out of her over dinner and drinks."

"More than I think I want," Brunelle hazarded a guess.

"And more than you can take," Casey raised a cautionary finger at him. "I don't care if you have dinner with her in exchange for information, but you better not do anything I do care about."

Brunelle smiled. "That's better."

"Don't worry, Romeo." Casey grabbed him by the chin. "I plan on keeping you around."

Brunelle's grin widened. He liked it when she said stuff

like that.

"Now, though," Casey opened Sabine's case file, "let's see what's in here."

Brunelle sat down next to her on the couch in their hotel room. This wasn't something you read out in public. It was a beautiful day and the late afternoon sun streamed in through the curtains, backlighting Casey's curls in a gilded glow. Sometimes there was nothing like the bird in the bush to make you appreciate the one in your hand.

"It's all in German, isn't it?" he asked.

"Mm-hmm," Casey confirmed, eyes glued to the file.

"You're not going to translate it out loud, word-for-word as you read, are you?" he followed up.

"That would be terrible," Casey said, still without looking up.

Brunelle agreed. He stood up. "I'm gonna go make us a couple of drinks. We still have some champagne in the fridge, right?"

Another "Mm-hmm" and Brunelle excused himself to the kitchen. He was in no hurry. It was a thick file. He could wait for the summary at the end. It took a lot less time to pour a couple of glasses of champagne than examine a murder case file, so Brunelle considered what he might do to pass the time while Casey did her part. He was debating between watching the TV on mute (it was in German anyway) or looking out the window at passersby, trying to guess their destinations. He walked back into the main room, set Casey's drink next to her, and picked up the remote. He didn't really care where anyone was going right then.

But he didn't get a chance to turn on the TV.

"So, this is interesting," Casey commented, raising her

chin but not her eyes from the papers in front of her.

Ah, it's going to be like this, Brunelle realized. He set the remote control back down. "What is?"

"Didn't Dieter tell us he didn't know that Ginkel and Ferensz knew each other?" Casey finally looked up at Brunelle as she asked the question.

Brunelle considered for a moment. "I think so." He took a sip of his champagne. "I mean, when we told him, he didn't say he already knew it, right?"

"Right," Casey agreed. "But I'm reading his report right now, and he definitely knew Ginkel worked at both Château Wunder and Spa Balibai."

"Well, that doesn't necessarily mean Ginkel and Ferensz knew each other." Brunelle shrugged. "Not everyone knows their boss, right? Especially at a place with a lot of employees."

Casey frowned. "It's not that big of a place."

"But why would he lie to us about that?" Brunelle asked.

"Maybe he knew we were snooping around the theater office," Casey suggested.

Brunelle thought for a moment. "That's a *non sequitur*."

"Hey." Casey jabbed a finger toward his face. "No Latin, lawyer boy. That's a rule."

Brunelle laughed. "That is most definitely not a rule. You date a lawyer, *ipso facto* you get Latin. *Res ipsa loquitur*."

"Stop," Casey warned. "I have a gun."

"Anyway," Brunelle shook his head at her, "I just mean, knowing we were at the theater isn't a reason to act surprised that Ginkel and Ferensz knew each other. One doesn't follow the other."

"Maybe he wanted to throw us off the trail," Casey suggested.

"Didn't he kind of invite us onto the trail?" Brunelle recalled.

Casey frowned. "Oh, yeah." She looked down at the file again. "That makes it even weirder."

"*Arguendo*," Brunelle replied. "*Nunc pro tunc.*"

"I will shoot you," Casey said without looking up again. "Don't test me. I know the cops here."

"You know one cop here," Brunelle reminded her, "and he doesn't appear to trust you."

Casey nodded. "He's probably just being careful. He doesn't actually know us. We might be useful to bounce ideas off of, but maybe it's smart of him to hold off sharing too many details of an active murder investigation with a couple of foreigners he just met."

"Yeah…" Brunelle considered. "Which makes this whole thing even harder to understand." He tapped the case file. "Sabine seems like she's at least as smart as Dieter, probably smarter. Smarter than me anyway."

"*Res ipsa loquitur*," Casey replied with a grin.

"Ha," Brunelle replied dryly. "So, if it's smarter not to tell us everything, why would Sabine give us, well, everything?"

Casey closed the file on her thumb and smiled at her boyfriend. "Maybe she's expecting you'll give her everything in return. *Biggus dickus.*"

Brunelle ran a hand over his face. "You're really going to enjoy this, aren't you?"

"That's how life is, Davey," she replied. "You can't always control what happens, but you can control whether you enjoy it."

Brunelle considered for a moment. He took a long drink of champagne. Then he pointed at Casey. "That," he said, "is total bullshit."

CHAPTER 19

It would be difficult not to enjoy dinner at a luxury restaurant with a beautiful woman, but Brunelle was determined to try.

Casey escorted him to the Edelstein. The plan was for her to wait a few doors down at the all-night café and pastry shop, then do a debriefing there over *Kaffee* and *Strüdel* immediately after the dinner. It would let them go over everything Sabine said while it was still fresh in Brunelle's mind. It would also keep anyone from going home with anyone else, except for the two people who were already sharing a hotel room.

"Don't do anything I wouldn't do," Casey gave him a peck on the cheek. "But definitely do everything I would do."

Brunelle cocked his head. "Like what?"

"Like gathering information," Casey answered. "Be a detective, but be undercover. Interrogate her without letting her know she's being interrogated."

Brunelle nodded. "I can do that."

Casey smiled at him and patted his cheek. "No, you can't, honey. But try anyway."

"Really?" Brunelle opened his hands at her. "That's the pep talk?"

"And don't fuck her," Casey added. "Now, go get 'em, tiger."

Brunelle shook his head. "Thanks, coach." Then he grabbed the oversized door handle to the restaurant and entered into his dinner date with Sabine Ehrenwald.

The restaurant was dimly lit, decorated in red velvet and gold accents, with wait staff in formal black and white attire. It looked like what a person who had never been to a fancy restaurant would think a fancy restaurant would look like.

The *maître d'*, a tall, thin man with tight skin and black eyes, greeted him with some German phrase Brunelle knew in advance he wouldn't understand.

"English?" Brunelle tried. Apparently, the German word sounded almost, but not quite, the same, so he tried to add what sounded like a German accent to it. The kind of German accent a person who had never heard a German accent would think a German accent would sound like.

The *maître d'* forced a smile of large teeth and pale gums. "Of course, sir. Do you have a reservation?"

"I'm meeting someone," Brunelle explained.

"Who would that be?" the man asked.

"Um," Brunelle raised a hand over his head. "She's about this tall, black hair, thin. Very attractive."

The grin calcified. "Of course, sir. And what is the name of this very attractive woman?"

"Sabine," answered Sabine Ehrenwald, stepping out of nowhere to rescue Brunelle from his efforts to find her. She met his description: tall, black hair, and outright stunning in a little black dress and heels. She grabbed the back of Brunelle's arm—

hard. "He is with me," she said in English, before saying something else in German that made the *maître d'*s smile suddenly become genuinely mirthful.

She steered Brunelle toward the seating section. "You are late."

Brunelle looked at his watch. It was exactly 7:00 p.m. "I'm right on time," he protested, his arm still in her vise-like grip.

Sabine chuckled, but only very slightly. "We have a saying in Germany." She let go of his arm as they reached their small square table in the corner a little past the bar. "Early is on time, on time is late, and late is unacceptable."

She pulled out her chair and sat down, all in one vicious movement.

"That's, uh," Brunelle resisted the urge to rub the back of his arm as he sought the right word, "intense."

Sabine scoffed and rolled her eyes. "Sit down. We have much to discuss."

It wasn't the same flirty vibe he was getting from her the previous day, but there was still something forcefully seductive about her demeanor. As if he might need medical attention when she was through with him, but it would have been worth it. He shook his head slightly and sat down opposite her.

"Thank you," she said.

"For sitting down?" Brunelle ventured. He felt like he was trying to jump on a moving train that was speeding up.

"No," Sabine answered. "For saying I am very attractive."

"Oh," Brunelle had already forgotten that. The train was pulling away. "I was, um, just trying to describe…uh, you're welcome."

He thought she might return the compliment, but she did not. "You have read my case file."

It wasn't exactly a question, but Brunelle knew to answer it anyway. "Yes. I read it."

Sabine's eyebrows lowered a bit, and she craned her sinewy neck to glance about his chair. "You did not bring it."

Again, not really a question. Again, he knew to provide an answer.

"Uh, no. I, uh, didn't want it to get food on it or something," he lied. In truth, Casey had it with her, to peruse at her leisure while he suffered through a gourmet meal with the Lady in Black. "It's back at my hotel room."

One of those lowered eyebrows shot up. "Oh, is it? That seems somewhat presumptuous of you, Davey."

"Oh!" Brunelle realized how it sounded. "No, I wasn't planning… That wasn't a plan, or anything. I just didn't bring it, is all. Sorry."

Sabine allowed herself a small grin. "Do not be sorry for telling a woman she is attractive and trying to get her to go to your hotel room. But," she unfurled a red-nailed finger at him, "that is not why we are here. Not now anyway."

"And why are we here?" Brunelle asked. He knew it was pathetic. He'd already forgotten Coach Casey's pep talk. But there was a lot going on. Thankfully, the waiter arrived with a bottle of wine.

A whole bunch of foreign language later, Sabine had procured two overly full glasses of red wine and ordered both of their entrees. She neither asked Brunelle what he wanted nor told him what he would be getting. It was kind of hot.

"We are here," Sabine picked up the conversation exactly where they had left off upon the arrival of the waiter, "for you to help me win this case."

"Right, right." Brunelle frowned slightly. "So, how am I

supposed to do that exactly? From everything Dieter told me, you're an experienced prosecutor. I'm not sure how I can help you, especially when I practice in a totally different system than you."

Sabine didn't reply immediately. Instead, she took a deep drink of her wine, which didn't exactly stain her already red lips, but layered a burgundy sateen onto them. When she set her glass down again, she produced that perfectly painted fingernail again. "First, it is precisely because you practice in a different system that I believe you can help me. Second, do not believe everything *Kommissaranwärter* Dieter Vorsburg tells you."

Brunelle leaned forward. "Why is that?"

"Why is what?" Sabine narrowed her eyes at him.

"What you just said," Brunelle prompted.

"Which thing I just said?" Sabine answered. "I said two things. You are very confusing."

"I've heard that before," Brunelle allowed. "The second one, about Dieter. Why shouldn't I believe him?"

Sabine smiled again at him. "Have you not already determined this for yourself? Did you read my case file? I'm beginning to think you did not."

"Well, I didn't read it," Brunelle admitted. "I can't read German. But Casey translated it for me."

"Hmmpf," Sabine sniffed. "Let us not talk about your traveling companion."

My bed companion, Brunelle thought, *but fine.*

"Tell me what you think about Dieter," Sabine pressed on, "now that you have read, one way or another, my case file."

Brunelle took a moment. Being interrogated without knowing you're being interrogated could be a two-way street. "I'm not sure I know enough about the case to say for sure. He did tell us that you ordered him not to question Ginkel when he was arrested. Is that true?"

Another pause, another drink of wine, another grin—but a cold one. "Let us talk about how you can help me. You Americans, you are used to defendants not speaking to detectives, yes? 'You have the right to remain silent' and all that, am I correct?"

Brunelle shrugged. "Most of them talk anyway, even after you tell them they should shut up. Everyone thinks they can talk their way out of it. They're wrong. If you're in a police interrogation room and they're reading you your rights, it's way too late to talk your way out of anything."

"But what do you do when the suspect does not answer questions?" Sabine argued. "How do you argue that it is evidence of their guilt? What is your big, theatrical, American argument that you use to convince the jury the suspect is guilty because he would not talk to the police?"

Brunelle tipped his head slightly. "I don't argue that," he answered. "I can't."

Sabine's expression became puzzled. "What do you mean you can't? Obviously, the suspect did not answer questions because he knew the answers would make him look guilty. Do you leave it at that, or is there something more? I need the strongest possible argument for this case. But I am accustomed to arguing to experienced judges, not uneducated jurors. How do you explain it in the simplest but strongest way?"

Brunelle shook his head. "I just told you, I can't argue that. I'm not allowed to. Our constitution says a criminal defendant has a right to remain silent. That right doesn't mean much if I can argue that exercising it means they're guilty."

Sabine pushed back in her chair and let out a long, loud

sigh. "I am not an idiot, Davey. I understand that argument. I know the defense will claim it is an empty right if it can be used against them. That is why I am asking you. I do not need the obvious argument. I need the subtle argument, the sneaky argument. I need the argument an American prosecutor makes to a jury. I need the argument that convinces the jury to convict even though the judge would not accept such an argument."

Brunelle took a beat to appraise his dinner companion. Finally, he asked, "Are you serious?"

Sabine leaned forward again. "I am very serious. Deadly serious. A man was murdered."

Brunelle rolled his eyes slightly at the dramatic reply. He shrugged. "I'm sorry, but I can't help you. We don't argue that. We can't. If I made any sort of argument like that, the judge would declare a mistrial. We would have to start all over again. If it was really bad, the case could even be dismissed."

Sabine laughed. "They would dismiss a murder case?" she scoffed.

"If it was bad enough," Brunelle insisted. "In fact, sneaky would be worse. It would show an intent to violate someone's rights and a desire to get away with it. I could lose my license for something like that."

Sabine sniffed at him. "Do not think we do not also have rules here? That defendants do not also have rights here? A suspect does not have to answer questions, but the judge will know that he refused, and we all know what that means. So, in America, do you simply tell the jury that he refused to talk but then hope they draw the proper conclusion?"

"No." Brunelle shook his head. "We can't even tell them the cops tried to ask questions. We just pretend they never even attempted to interview the defendant."

Sabine's eyes widened. "You lie to the jury? You let them believe your police officers didn't even try? That your police officers are incompetent?"

"Well, in our defense," Brunelle offered a timid grin, "if not interviewing a suspect is incompetent, isn't that what happened in your case?"

Sabine wasn't smiling anymore. She definitely wasn't laughing. "So, that is it, then?" she barked. "You have nothing? Nothing for me at all?"

Before Brunelle could answer, the waiter brought their food. He set down two plates filled with some sort of meat and some sort of potatoes both covered in some sort of sauce.

"I don't know about 'nothing'." Brunelle gestured at their meals. "We'll always have, um, whatever this is."

"It is pork," Sabine grumbled.

"Of course," Brunelle said. He'd been in Germany long enough to know the odds were pretty good that any given slice of meat was probably pork. "So, we'll always have pork."

"You will have it as long as it takes you to eat it," Sabine muttered as she began cutting her pork chop. "Then we will be done, and you may leave."

Brunelle frowned. "That's it? That's all you wanted?"

Sabine looked up from her plate. "It may not be all I wanted, Mr. Brunelle, but it was the first thing. Without that, I see no need to proceed further."

Brunelle looked down at his own meal. He wasn't a big fan of eating things he didn't recognize. Then again, it was a fancy restaurant, so the chef was probably pretty good. He picked up his own knife and fork.

"This is going to be a long meal if we don't talk to each other," he said.

Sabine looked him in the eye, finished chewing her bite, swallowed it, then took a drink of wine to wash it down. "It will take even longer if we do talk to each other."

Brunelle could hardly argue with that. He cut off a slice of pork and gave it a try. As expected, it was pretty good.

"But let us leave it at this," Sabine suddenly said, startling Brunelle a bit. "If you do have something helpful to say, you may contact me. Perhaps something will come to you after you consider our conversation."

"Our conversation?" Brunelle questioned. "You mean tonight? Like, the thirty words we've said to each other? That's not really a conversation."

Sabine nodded. "I was right. This is going to take longer if we continue talking."

Brunelle looked at her for several moments, but she didn't lift her head from her plate again. He shrugged and decided to eat as fast as he could as well. The quicker he ate, the sooner he could spend time with a woman who actually liked him.

* * *

"How was dinner?" Casey asked as Brunelle walked into the café and gave her a kiss on the cheek. She checked the time on her phone. "That was quick," she realized.

Brunelle nodded and took the seat next to her. They were at a counter at the front window facing out at the street and its passersby. "She's not much of a conversationalist, it turns out."

"What did you find out?" Casey asked.

"Not much," Brunelle shrugged. "She wanted me to help her craft an argument about why the defendant's refusal to answer questions should he held against him as evidence of guilt. When I told her we weren't allowed to do that in the U.S. so I couldn't really help her, she declared we were done talking and told me to hurry up and finish my schnitzel, or whatever it was she ordered for me."

"She ordered your dinner for you?" Casey laughed.

"That's what you took out of that?" Brunelle shook his head. "That was the least weird part, actually. It wasn't like I could have read the menu."

"Good point," Casey conceded. "Did you learn anything else?"

Brunelle thought for a minute. "She doesn't trust Dieter."

Casey raised an eyebrow. "Oh, really? What makes you say that?"

"She told me not to believe him," Brunelle answered. "So, that was pretty straightforward. It was when I told her Dieter said it was her who ordered him not to interview Ginkel."

"So, she denied that?" Casey asked.

Brunelle considered for a moment. "Not directly. She just told me not to believe what Dieter said about it."

"He said she told him not to interview the subject." Casey patted the case file in front of her. "It was very clear."

"Yeah, well, apparently you can't trust the lead detective," Brunelle said.

"Or the lead prosecutor," Casey added.

"Who else can we talk to?" Brunelle mused. "Who else would know what happened when Ginkel got arrested, but isn't the detective or the prosecutor?"

They both sat in silence for several moments, staring out the window and considering their options. After those several moments, they looked at each other and nodded.

"The defense attorney," they said in unison.

CHAPTER 20

It was too late to just go accost some defense attorney. More importantly, they didn't know who that attorney was yet, so they couldn't have even if they'd wanted to—which they kind of did. It would have to wait until morning.

Breakfast that next morning was an assortment of rolls and smoked meat from the café next door and two cups of coffee each, the second helpings in to-go cups. It was nice enough weather and a short enough walk. There may have been a murder to solve—well, solve *more*—but there were still sights to see. And you weren't supposed to take coffee on the subway anyway.

Their first stop was the courthouse. Ginkel's attorney might be in there somewhere, but poking their heads inside each courtroom looking for the right attorney—someone who just sort of looked like they might represent a ginkel—would be like looking for a *Nadel* in a *Heuhafen*. Instead, they made their way across the main lobby to the clerk's office. Court systems and processes and procedures might be different from country to country, but they all had one thing in common: lots and lots of paper.

Everything of legal significance had to documented, recorded, stored, indexed, and generally accessible. Written proof in case there was a challenge or claim later. Who owned what piece of property. Who was married to whom. What crime Mathias Ginkel was charged with. And who his lawyer was.

"Here it is," Casey announced as she flipped to the correct document in the file she had checked out from the clerk.

Brunelle was admiring the paintings on the wall since he couldn't actually read the file in the matter of *The People of the Federal Republic of Germany versus Mathias German-Middle-Name Ginkel*. He turned back to his girlfriend, eyebrows appropriately raised to encourage the lawyer's name without actually having to say anything out loud.

"Jürgen Schweitzer," Casey announced. *"Anwalt für den Angeklagten.* Attorney for the accused."

"The first two words were his name, right?" Brunelle clarified. "I've heard the name Jurgen before, I think."

"Jürgen," Casey corrected his pronunciation.

"Jurgen," Brunelle tried to repeat.

"The u has an umlaut," Casey advised. "Jüüürgen"

"Are we really doing this?" Brunelle shook his head at her. "I don't even know what an umlaut is."

"It's the two dots over the vowel," Casey explained.

"Like Mötley Crüe?" Brunelle asked.

Casey became stone faced. "No. Nothing like Mötley Crüe."

"Okay, whatever," Brunelle waved the tangent aside. "So, Juuurgen Schnitzel is his lawyer. Perfect. Now we just need to find him. It is a him, right? Juuurgen is a dude's name, right?"

"Jürgen is," Casey answered. "I don't know about Juurgen." She rolled her eyes at him, but then pointed at the document in the file. "This is his office address. It's not too far from here, I don't think."

"Near the courthouse." Brunelle nodded. "That makes sense."

Casey jotted the address down on a piece of scrap paper and closed the file. "Come on," she said as she closed the file and took it back to the clerk's counter. "If we leave now, we might be able to catch him before lunch."

* * *

"He just left for lunch," Casey translated the information from Schweitzer's receptionist.

Brunelle frowned, but Casey asked another question and got another unintelligible (to Brunelle) response.

"He's at the Italian place right around the corner," Casey announced. "We should be able to catch him."

Casey offered a *"Danke!"* to the secretary—one of the few German words Brunelle did understand—and hurried him out of Schweitzer's office. "She said it takes him a full hour to eat."

"Because he likes to relax?" Brunelle ventured.

Casey thought for a moment. "No, that wasn't the impression I got. It was more like, it takes that long to eat it all."

The restaurant was named 'Casa Mia' and it was right around the corner from Schweitzer's office building. Even with what little information the receptionist had given them, Schweitzer was easy to identify. At a table against the windows, several plates and bowls of pasta and bread and meat before him, sat one of the largest human beings Brunelle had ever seen, at least in person.

It wasn't that the man was obese, although he was definitely rotund. He was simply enormous—at least 6'6" and easily over 300 pounds. He rested thick, meaty hands on either side of his table, seemingly casting the furniture in miniature, like a father getting ready for his daughter's tea party. Thinning black hair was combed over a bald, pink, sweaty head. And perched on a putty-like nose were a pair of gold wire-rimmed glasses that looked like they might have been meant to be fashionably small but probably only looked small compared to the humungous man wearing them.

"Herr Schweitzer?" Casey approached the man.

Schweitzer looked up at the sound of his name. "*Ja?*" His glasses made his eyes look even smaller in his puffy face, completing the look of a prize hog in a tailored suit—a character from a Beatrix Potter story.

Casey followed up with some more German. Brunelle picked out the word *Englisch* again and knew she was apologizing for Brunelle's own lack of language ability.

"*Ja*, I can speak English," Schweitzer switched over. The usual thinly veiled derision for having to do so was lacking from his tone. Brunelle liked him already. "Would you care to join me for lunch?"

Brunelle glanced at the small table engulfed by Schweitzer and wondered, *Where?* But instead he said, "Yes, thank you very much."

Casey took the chair opposite Schweitzer and Brunelle pulled one over from the table next to them. He had to sit sort of sideways between the tables.

"So, you are American lawyers?" Schweitzer started, breathing heavily between sentences. "What can I do for you?"

"He's the lawyer." Casey pointed at Brunelle. "I'm a police officer. A detective actually. My name is Casey Emory. This is Dave Brunelle."

Brunelle extended a hand that was swallowed by

Schweitzer's own grip. "Davey," he corrected. In for a penny, in for a pound. "And I'm a prosecutor."

"*Staatsanwalt*," Casey translated.

"Ah." Schweitzer nodded his head. "So, why do an American detective and an American prosecutor want to speak with a German attorney who represents people charged with crimes?"

"We're interested in one particular person," Brunelle explained.

"Charged with one particular crime," Casey added. "Murder."

"Ah," Schweitzer said again, nodding his large head. He may have looked like a bespectacled hog in a business suit, but he seemed to be an intelligent, thoughtful hog. "I have several such clients right now, but somehow I suspect you are interested in the Mathias Ginkel matter, yes?"

Casey and Brunelle traded glances.

"How did you know?" Brunelle asked.

"Because the other cases are not very interesting," Schweitzer answered. "Also because American tourists named Davey Brunelle and Casey Emory are far more likely to go to Spa Balibai than the places where my other cases took place. But mostly because your names are in the police reports. You are the ones who found Mr. Ferensz's body, yes?"

"Um, yes," Brunelle practically admitted. "I'd forgotten about that."

"Me too," Casey agreed.

"In truth, I have been expecting you to contact me," Schweitzer added. "I was beginning to wonder what was taking you so long."

"You expect witnesses to contact you?" Brunelle was

surprised. Usually he did the contacting, as trial approached.

"*Nein,*" Schweitzer answered. "I expected two Americans, employed in law enforcement and witnesses to a murder, who have been seen consulting with the local police and prosecutors, and who have been conducting their own side investigation, to contact me."

Brunelle and Casey exchanged glances again.

"My only question," Schweitzer continued, "is whether you have finally come to see me because you have run out of leads for your investigation or because you have actually learned something valuable and are encouraged to continue."

"Okay, wait, wait, wait." Casey waved her hands at Schweitzer. "Let's back up. You said we've been 'seen' consulting with the local police and prosecutor. Seen by whom?"

Schweitzer raised an eyebrow above the rim of his glasses. "Am I wrong?"

"That's not the point," Casey returned.

Schweitzer shrugged, a massive movement that shook the table. "Perhaps, perhaps not. Why don't you ask me what you have come to ask me? Then I can decide whether I should tell you more than I already have."

It wasn't an unreasonable request, Brunelle thought. Schweitzer didn't owe them anything, and they had in fact come to ask him questions. He didn't have to agree to talk to them at all.

"Okay," Brunelle said. "Deal."

He looked to Casey. "You want to ask your question, or should I ask mine?"

Casey frowned slightly. They hadn't coordinated the questioning in advance. She didn't know what Brunelle's question was going to be, so she gave the smart answer. "I'll go first."

Brunelle nodded slightly. He knew she'd choose that option.

Casey leaned forward, although there wasn't really room for her to lean on the table. "Did Detective Vorsburg ever try to question your client, and if not, why not?"

Schweitzer smiled. "That's two questions, detective," he pointed out. "But I will answer them both. No, he did not, and no, I do not know why."

"The reports say the prosecutor told him not to," Casey reminded him.

"They do say that, yes," Schweitzer agreed. "I have read those reports. But I will repeat my answer. I do not know the real reason he did not question my client. I am simply glad for his decision."

Schweitzer turned to Brunelle. "Your question, *Herr Staatsanwalt*?"

Casey was caught up on procedure. Brunelle wanted the truth .

"Why did Ginkel murder Ferensz?"

Schweitzer's smile faltered, but only for a moment, then it actually grew larger. "Your question supposes many facts, Davey."

"If you answer it," Brunelle replied, "I know those facts are true."

Schweitzer nodded. "You are a lawyer, yes?"

"Yes," Brunelle agreed.

"You are an experienced lawyer, yes?"

"Yes again," Brunelle confirmed.

"Then you know I will not answer your question," Schweitzer said. "Even if I could."

Brunelle let his own cautious smile broaden a bit as well. "Then that answers at least part of it."

He turned to Casey. "Ginkel did kill Ferensz," he explained.

"Thank you, Sherlock," Casey huffed. "I could figure that out, too."

She looked again to Schweitzer. "So, are you going to tell us who's been going around 'seeing' us do stuff? It wouldn't be the same guys who attacked us in an alley behind Château Wunder, would it?"

"Attacked me," Brunelle put in.

"What?" Casey swung her head to him.

"Me," Brunelle repeated. "they attacked me. You had already run away by then."

"Really?" Casey asked, palms turned up.

"I'm just saying," Brunelle defended, his own hands raised.

Schweitzer was smiling again. "I like you two. So I will answer your question."

Casey gave Brunelle a 'told-you-so' look. He tried to counter with a 'nyah-nyah' look but wasn't sure he'd quite pulled it off.

"No," Schweitzer said. "No one was watching you when that happened. No one I know anyway. If they had been, you would not have been attacked."

Brunelle looked again to his girlfriend. He wasn't sure if they were done. She didn't seem sure either. But Schweitzer was.

"Now, if you will excuse me," he gestured toward the plates of still uneaten food before him, "I really do need to eat my lunch and get back to work."

CHAPTER 21

"That whole conversation with Schweitzer was kind of strange, don't you think?" Casey asked Brunelle as they ascended from the U-Bahn into the plaza behind the Brandenburg Gate. The subway stop wasn't right by their hotel, but it was right by a few of the landmarks they hadn't quite gotten around to seeing yet. The perfect opportunity to walk and talk.

Brunelle shrugged. "I don't know. He didn't tell us much, but he's not supposed to. I can respect he wants to keep his client confidences."

"No, no, not that," Casey replied. "The part about us being followed." She darted her head around at the crowded plaza.

"I think he said 'watched' not 'followed'," Brunelle recalled.

"Well, we can't be watched if we're not being followed," Casey pointed out. Her eyes narrowed as she scanned their surroundings. "It could be anyone."

"Anyone but Schweitzer," Brunelle remarked. "There's no way we wouldn't have noticed him. He's the size of a mountain."

Casey nodded. "That's true, and the only other two people we would recognize are Dieter and Sabine. I doubt either of them would bother following us."

"It does seem unlikely," Brunelle agreed. "Dieter would rather walk with us, and Sabine would rather walk away."

"So, it's someone we don't know," Casey concluded. "That's going to make it harder to identify them."

They had reached a side alley that led to the Gendarmenmarkt plaza, home of the not quite twin French Cathedral and German Cathedral, two beautifully ornate, domed churches facing each other across a cobblestoned plaza. Great sightlines to check if someone was following them, but a bit too open and crowded to know for sure. Still, the buildings were pretty.

"I agree," Brunelle said. "I always find it difficult to identify people I don't know."

"And have never seen," Casey added. "Or at least, we didn't know we saw them." She turned and looked over her shoulder again. "It could be any of these people."

"Or none of them," Brunelle said. "Probably none of them. We aren't doing anything interesting enough to bother following us. Unless maybe they wanted to snap a selfie in front of one of these churches."

Casey nodded for a few moments, silent in her thoughts. "That's it," she said after a moment.

"Ask our pursuer to take a selfie with us?" Brunelle questioned.

"No," Casey shook her head. "Although we should ask someone to take a picture of us. But you're right. We aren't doing anything interesting enough to want to follow us. And despite these beautifully restored landmarks, we aren't in a place interesting enough to want to monitor us."

Brunelle waited for more. There's wasn't any forthcoming. "Okay, so…" he prompted.

"So," Casey grinned, "we need to go somewhere and do something worth following. Then we'll know we're being followed, and we can turn the tables on them!"

"Turn the tables." Brunelle narrowed his eyes at her. "So, we follow them instead?"

Casey rolled her eyes. "No, silly." She sighed. "We confront them. Lead them down some dark, dead-end alley, then turn and confront them about who they are and why they're following us."

"Shouldn't we maybe confront them in a well-lit, open place, with lots of witnesses?" Brunelle suggested. "So they don't kill us or something? Just a thought."

"No," Casey assured him. She gestured around the plaza they were standing in. "Every witness is also a person to hide behind, a crowd to blend into. No, if we're going to figure out who's following us, we need to lead them so far away from anyone else, there will be no doubt who they are and what they're doing. Then, bam! We'll have them."

"Or bam! They shoot us," Brunelle countered.

Casey smiled. "Not if I shoot first. I brought my gun with me. I wasn't joking before when I said I had a gun."

"You brought a gun?" Brunelle had to stop himself from yelling. "Are you crazy? They have crazy strict gun control laws here."

"I'm a cop," Casey defended.

"Not here," Brunelle reminded her. "Here, you're a foreigner carrying an illegal firearm. I bet that's a crime here. I'm sure that's a crime here."

But Casey shrugged it off. "I followed all the proper procedures. I submitted my application to the German authorities well before we got on the plane."

"Did they approve it?" Brunelle asked.

"They didn't deny it," Casey answered. "I'm sure they would have, but time ran out. But no worries. It was in my checked luggage in a locked case. I declared it to the airline, and they were fine with it too. I am law enforcement, after all."

"Again, not here," Brunelle repeated. He sighed. "But I guess it's a good thing, since you're going to lead us into a dark, dead-end alleyway with God knows who right behind us."

"God may know who's been following us," Casey smiled again, "But after tonight, we're going to know too."

CHAPTER 22

"Château Wunder, take two!"

Casey frowned at Brunelle.

He tried again. "Château Wunder, redux!"

Casey kept frowning, but looked away.

"Château Wunder, the Revenge!" Brunelle whispered ominously. "How's that?"

"How about you be quiet?" Casey answered. She was in the same yellow dress she'd worn the first time they'd gone to the cabaret theater. "We're almost there. I thought you'd be happy to go back to this place."

Brunelle frowned himself. He was also in the same outfit; that suit was getting a lot of wear. "I'd be happier if we actually got tickets to the show," he complained. "I want to see how it ends."

"Worry about how our plan is going to end," Casey suggested.

"Your plan," Brunelle reminded her. "My plan was open, crowded, lots of witnesses. Your plan is dark alley with guns."

"One gun," Casey corrected.

Brunelle shrugged. "I hope you're right about that."

They turned the corner and Château Wunder came into view, its majestic turrets backlit by the setting sun. It was just as busy as the last time they'd come. Maybe even more so. This time they weren't running late. They had things to do before the show. The show they weren't going to anyway.

Casey led the way across the courtyard to the front entrance. Not because she was trying to walk ahead of him, but because Brunelle was hanging back. In part, to try to catch a glimpse of anyone who might be looking their way. But also because Casey looked really good in that yellow dress.

There was a small crowd milling about outside the front doors, mostly to smoke cigarettes, it seemed. Casey and Brunelle marched through the smokers and directly into the front lobby. It was more crowded there, as people stood in line for the will call window or waited for the rest of their party before heading deeper into the psychedelic light show of the main lobby.

Their secret admirer could have been any one of the other people surrounding them, or more likely, someone who was about to walk in after them, having maintained the respectful distance of a clandestine stalker. Accordingly, they took a spot in the will call line and waited, both for their turn at the window, and for their follower to enter the theater.

"Next!" is what Brunelle figured the translation was for whatever the young woman behind the will call window called out in German when it was their turn to approach.

What followed was all in German, but Brunelle knew the script. Casey played the obnoxious patron who lost her temper when the tickets she placed at will call (she never placed any tickets at will call) weren't there. The young woman played the part of the, well, the young woman getting yelled at by the obnoxious patron who lost her temper because her tickets weren't there.

Brunelle stood off to the side, becoming increasingly impressed at Casey's performance. He wasn't the only one. At least, he wasn't the only one watching—he was unsure whether anyone else was impressed. But everyone else in the front lobby had little choice but to turn their attention to the woman in the yellow dress yelling ever louder with each exchange. Brunelle didn't know the German word for 'manager' but he knew that was how the scene ended. When the young woman, on the verge of tears, finally got up from her seat and disappeared into the back, Brunelle knew the manager was on his way. Everyone else in the theater lobby knew it too.

Casey stepped back next to Brunelle and crossed her arms triumphantly. "She's getting the manager," she whispered.

"I figured," Brunelle acknowledged.

He glanced around the lobby, a bit sheepishly. Everyone had heard. And everyone looked irritated. Probably because it was delaying their own ability to pick up the tickets they had actually ordered. "I wonder if it will be—"

"Hans-Peter Oberflacher," announced the manager—*the* manager—as he stepped up to Casey and Brunelle, hand extended in greeting. Brunelle recognized the name from their ill-fated ransack of his office.

Casey shook Oberflacher's hand first, even as the manager said something besides his name, which meant Brunelle couldn't understand it. But he knew how to shake a hand and did so after Casey released her grasp.

Casey said something along the lines of, 'My boyfriend doesn't speak German. Can we do this in English?' (Brunelle had heard it enough times to pick out the key words), and Oberflacher obliged effortlessly.

"Of course," he effused. "Now, how can I help you?"

He was tall and thin, with short but stylish gray hair and wrinkles around his eyes and mouth. Dark brown, almost black eyes hid behind tortoise-shell glasses. His shiny, dark gray suit was at once classic and modern, and perfectly tailored for his trim build.

Casey took the lead, again according to script. "We are shocked and dismayed, *Herr* Oberflacher. Your theater has lost our tickets and your employee refuses to provide us with replacements. We demand that you make this right."

Oberflacher glanced over at the will call window. The young woman had returned to her seat and offered her boss nothing more than a bewildered shrug.

"You are certain." Oberflacher asked, "that you made arrangements to pick up your tickets at will call?"

Casey gasped and put her fists on her hips. "Are you calling me a liar, *Herr* Oberflacher?" Her voice was definitely raised. People were definitely watching.

Oberflacher smiled nervously. "No, no, madame. Of course not. It's only —"

"You had better not be calling me a liar, *Herr* Oberflacher," Casey lifted those fists and crossed her arms at him. "Is it because we're Americans? Is that it? Or is it because I'm —"

"No, no!" Oberflacher interrupted. "Of course not." He glanced over at the ticket window then back again. "The show is sold out tonight. We are sold out every night. But I may be able to do something..." Although he didn't seem certain what that something would be. Perhaps squeeze them in to stand in the back again, although Casey wasn't throwing off the vibe of a woman who would be satisfied with standing in the back.

"Well, I'm glad you're sold out every night, *Herr* Oberflacher." Casey's heavy sarcasm was understandable even to a non-native English speaker. "But I don't really care about any other night. My boyfriend and I just want to spend our Tuesday night at your theater, with the tickets we paid for, in the seats we purchased. How hard is that?"

Oberflacher's head tilted sharply. "Tuesday? Did you say Tuesday?"

Casey rolled her eyes and huffed. "Yes, *Herr* Oberflacher. Tuesday." Then, to be even more obnoxious, she went ahead and translated it for him, "*Dienstag.*"

Oberflacher stood up a bit straighter. Brunelle hadn't even noticed he was slouching forward until he stopped doing it. "But today is Wednesday," Oberflacher explained, obviously pleased to do so. And he could translate too: "*Mittwoch.*"

Acting wasn't simply reading the lines on the page. It was also facial expressions and body language. But Casey had written that particular script, so she was prepared to be mortified. "Wednesday?" she almost whispered. "Are you sure?"

She looked to Brunelle, the cue for him to shrug. She had given him a part, but it wasn't a speaking role.

Casey looked back to Oberflacher. "Oh," she squeaked. "Never mind."

She looked around sheepishly at the crowd staring them down. Enough of them understood English to know what had been said. The rest understood the difference between *Dienstag* and *Mittwoch* and could extrapolate.

Oberflacher was obviously pleased with the result, but he was still a businessman, and a host. "Perhaps we can see if there are tickets available for later this week, if you will still be in town."

But Casey waved away the offer. "Oh no, no, no. That's alright. That's fine. We're fine. We're good. We're going to go now, I think."

She turned and took Brunelle's arm. He resisted the urge to break character and ask about those tickets later in the week—he really did want to see Act II—and let Casey pull him out of the lobby, through the irritated crowd, and past, they hoped, their stalker.

The smokers outside had mostly dissipated, the show about to begin. Brunelle and Casey walked out into the night, holding hands, the hard soles of their shoes clacking off the cobblestones. They pretended to engage in small talk, but actually perked their ears up to catch any sound of a third pair of footsteps trailing after them.

They were almost completely out of the courtyard before they heard them.

Dull thumps, not sharp clacks. He was smart, not wearing loud shoes, but as they all got farther from the theater, there were less people and less noise and the footfall of rubber on stone was barely discernible.

Even over the rush of blood suddenly pounding in Brunelle's ears.

Parts I and II of Casey's plan had worked. They had made a scene. They had drawn out their pursuer. Brunelle only hoped Part III would turn out equally well—the part that involved the firearm. What could go wrong?

They hastened their steps as they turned another corner down a deserted alleyway. The foot thumps behind them hastened as well.

What could go wrong? Brunelle asked himself again. They'd find out soon enough.

CHAPTER 23

Large cities are full of people; that's what makes them large cities. But there are always those out of the way places the businessmen avoid and the tourists don't know about. Dark streets and back alleys where the only people are those who are forced to live there, and even they would rather be someplace else.

Berlin was no different, and it didn't take long for Brunelle and Casey to travel from the happy crowded plaza in front of the lively cabaret to a desolate maze of back alleys designed to house those who hung on by working out of the back kitchens and cleaning closets of those lively cabarets.

The alleyways were narrow, and it was hard to know exactly where they were, despite having planned their route via the map app on Casey's phone. They hesitated at each intersection, taking a moment to confirm their path. Their pursuer had no such need to pause. He didn't need to know the way; he only needed to know their way.

"Our plan is working," Brunelle whispered, the three sets of footsteps clearly audible in the still night.

"My plan," Casey reminded him, one eye on her phone, the other on the cobblestones ahead. She grabbed his arm and pulled him down another, even narrower walkway. "Turn here."

The footsteps behind them were getting closer. Brunelle thought they somehow seemed heavier than his. Plodding. Large. Whoever it was, they weren't small.

Great. Brunelle frowned as he was pulled deeper down the winding alleyway. If he remembered the map correctly, they were almost to their destination: a hopelessly isolated cul-de-sac. He suddenly questioned why Casey was the only one with a gun.

Two more corners and they had arrived, not quite running, but not just walking anymore either. It was a little more than just the end of the alley, widening slightly at the terminus. There were no windows on the ground level, just a pair of locked doors and brick walls towering high enough to block out the light of the moon. Dark shadows angled across the miniature courtyard, casting almost everything into blackness. Casey grabbed Brunelle one last time and pulled him into one of the doorways. It was deep enough to hide the both of them, and dark enough to conceal them completely. Their footsteps had stopped, but there was one set still echoing off the stones. And they were almost upon them.

Then they stopped.

Right in front of them.

It was dark, but it wasn't impossible to see, especially from their vantage point in the doorway, looking out from a darker place to a somewhat less dark place. Brunelle had been half-right. The person following them wasn't just large, he was enormous. For a moment, Brunelle thought maybe it was Schweitzer after all, but after that moment, the enormous, heavy-footed shadow person spun and darted his hand into their doorway. He wasn't just large; he was fast. And he had Casey's wrist.

She screamed as she was yanked out of the doorway, her toes scraping at the pavement, and her gun clattering across the cobblestones.

Brunelle lunged after her, but it was too late. They were cornered, Casey hanging by her wrist, and Brunelle unarmed.

It definitely wasn't Schweitzer. It was how Schweitzer would have looked like if he were in the shape of an Olympic weightlifter. This guy didn't eat entire pizzas for lunch. But he looked like he was ready to eat them for dinner.

Brunelle caught a glimpse of the gun lying against the wall. He scrambled over and snatched it off the ground. But he was a lawyer, not a cop. Guns weren't his thing. To the extent he ever handled them, it was in a courtroom. Bullets and magazine in separate bags, with a lock on the trigger and a zip tie through the barrel. Nonetheless he leveled the weapon at their pursuer-turned-attacker.

"Let her go."

CHAPTER 24

"He probably doesn't speak English," Casey said after Brunelle issued his firearm-backed order.

"Really?" Brunelle was incredulous. "You're still translating?"

"Hey, do you want him to let me go or not?" Casey argued.

"I think my gun is translating just fine, thank you," Brunelle retorted.

"My gun," Casey reminded him. "And clear instructions are vital when you have a weapon trained on a subject."

"Oh my God." Brunelle couldn't believe it. "You're giving me a lesson in police tactics right now?"

The man holding Casey's wrist looked confused. In the half-light, Brunelle could tell he was young, with a mop of reddish-brown hair and a thin, scraggly beard trying to grow on his cheeks. He glanced back and forth between Casey and Brunelle several times, then frowned, still ahold of Casey's arm.

"*Ich bin Heiko,*" he said finally.

"What did he say?" Brunelle demanded, gun still pointed

at them.

"Oh, now you want a translation?" Casey replied. "He said his name is Heiko."

"I don't give a fuck what his name is," Brunelle fairly shouted back. "Tell him to let you go or I'll shoot him."

"No, you'll shoot me," Casey said. "Lower the gun, cowboy. I think I can handle this, but not as long as you're threatening to kill him."

Brunelle hesitated. But he trusted Casey. He lowered the handgun. Not all the way, but enough to get the message across.

Then Casey said something to the man in German. Brunelle didn't understand, but comprehension began to form on their pursuer's face. After a few sentences, the man lowered Casey back onto her feet and let go of her wrist.

He turned to Brunelle and put up his hands. *"Schieß Heiko nicht."*

Brunelle was starting to pick up a few words, especially *'nicht'*, plus Heiko was a gimme and *'schieß'* was a cognate. Heiko's hands up was also kind of a giveaway. Fifty percent of language was context.

"He said don't shoot him, right?" Brunelle asked Casey.

"Hey, there's hope for you yet," Casey teased. "Put the gun away, Dave. I'll handle this."

Then she did. She talked to big, bad Heiko for several minutes. It was too fast, with a lot more words than *'nicht'*, so Brunelle had no hope of understanding any of it. Instead, he watched their faces and observed as Casey formed that bond a really good detective could form with a potentially dangerous, but ultimately human, subject.

Casey turned to Brunelle. "He's a friend of Ginkel's"

That surprised Brunelle. He wasn't sure why anything

should surprise him anymore—he was standing in a deserted alleyway in Berlin, a loaded gun in his hand, while his girlfriend spoke German to the Incredible Hulk—but that surprised him.

"Ginkel?" he repeated. "Why would Ginkel have him follow us?"

"I don't think it was Ginkel," Casey explained. "I think it was Schweitzer. He told Ginkel about us from the reports. He thinks we can help Ginkel, but he was worried about our safety, so they asked Heiko to follow us. This was his first night on the job."

Brunelle rolled his eyes. "Great job."

Casey shrugged. "It could have been worse. He saw the gun in my hand and reacted. He was just protecting himself."

"And us?" Brunelle asked. "That's the plan? A huge goon following us in case some busboys attack us again?"

"He's not a goon," Casey defended. "He's a Heiko." She patted Heiko's thick arm. "Schweitzer thinks we have bigger concerns than some angry busboys."

"Why should Schweitzer care about us?" Brunelle wondered.

"He probably doesn't," Casey guessed. "But he cares about Ginkel, and he thinks we can help him."

"Can we?" Brunelle asked.

Casey thought for a moment. "I'm not sure," she admitted. "But now I want to."

CHAPTER 25

Heiko proved to be a more likeable escort than stalker. He walked Brunelle and Casey back to their hotel, in case there really was anything, or anyone, to worry about. The conversation was minimal, in part because Brunelle couldn't participate, and in part because Heiko wasn't much of a talker. Big and German and friends with an accused murderer, but not much in the way of explanations. Ginkel asked him to watch out for Brunelle and Casey, so he did. A good friend ...of an accused murderer.

That meant the real answers were going to have to come from someplace else. That someplace else, or someone else, was obvious. The time and location were obvious too. Noon at the Italian eatery around the corner from the Law Offices of Jürgen Schweitzer.

"I thought I might see you again," Schweitzer greeted as they approached.

"I would think so," Brunelle answered. "After sending someone to follow us."

"Watch out for us," Casey corrected. "At least, that's what he claimed."

"Seemed legit," Brunelle admitted. "I mean, after he assaulted you."

"Self-defense," Casey suggested.

Brunelle accepted that with a shrug.

"I have no idea what you two are talking about," Schweitzer said with a shake of his head.

"Oh, really?" Brunelle scoffed as he pulled out a chair and sat down sort of next to the large attorney. Then, seriously. "Wait. Really?"

"No idea?" Casey reiterated. "You don't know about Heiko?"

"Heiko?" Schweitzer asked. "Who is Heiko?"

"The goon you sent after us last night," Brunelle answered.

"Dave, seriously." Casey frowned at him. "He's not a goon."

"Dave?" Heiko questioned. "I thought it was Davey."

"Let's focus," Casey suggested. "Do you know a friend of Mathias Ginkel named Heiko?"

"I don't know any of Mathias's friends," Schweitzer answered. "I am his lawyer, not his mommy."

"So, you didn't send anyone to follow us?" Brunelle pressed.

Schweitzer waited a moment before answering. He took a sip from his water glass and looked to be considering taking a bite from his lunch, before finally speaking. "Let me answer your question with another question. Why do you think I sent someone to follow you? Is it because someone followed you? That's a start, of course. But why must it be I who sent him? Why not Mathias himself?"

"I'm pretty sure Heiko told us you sent him," Brunelle

answered. He looked to Casey. "Isn't that right?"

Casey hesitated. "I'm not sure now exactly. He didn't say much. I may have inferred the part about who sent him. It didn't make sense that the suspect would send someone. I mean, how does Ginkel even communicate that to Heiko?"

"There are ways, of course," Schweitzer reminded them. "Visitors, other friends, and the like. But the interesting thing is that you chose to ignore those possibilities in favor of assuming it was me. It was someone with power, with authority, with standing. Someone," he waved a hand at his lunch guests, "like you."

Brunelle looked at Casey for her reaction. It was pretty much the same as his: 'What the hell is he talking about?'

"Go on," Brunelle encouraged.

Schweitzer leaned back in his chair and steepled his fingers. "We are lawyers, you and I, yes, Davey?"

Brunelle nodded.

"And you are a police officer, yes, Casey?"

"Detective," she reminded him, "but yes."

"Yes, a detective," Schweitzer accepted the correction. "Even better. So, you, Detective Casey, you look at the world as it is and try to imagine the world as it was. You find a bullet casing, and you imagine the shot. You stand over a dead man, and you imagine his death. You take your facts, and you imagine more facts. Facts that make sense, at least to you. But part of what allows them to make sense to you is that they also make sense to others."

Schweitzer turned to Brunelle. "But you and I, we sell those facts, don't we? We do not try to invent new facts. We take the facts the detectives give us, and we explain them to others. We convince others to believe the facts, or at least the facts we want them to believe, and we try to convince them not to believe the facts which we find, let us say, inconvenient."

Brunelle considered Schweitzer's words. He wasn't wrong. There was something comforting in knowing that lawyering was similar no matter where one practiced.

Brunelle nodded. "That sounds right to me."

"Of course it is," Schweitzer responded. "I will be making such arguments the day after tomorrow when the judge decides whether there is sufficient evidence to allow Mathias's case to proceed to trial. The judge will review all of the government's evidence and decide whether the case will go forward. But even then, the judge will assess my arguments not only by the words I say but also by the role I play. I am unlikely to prevail."

Schweitzer pointed at Brunelle. "Let me ask you the important question, Davey. Perhaps you can help me to win my hearing."

Brunelle raised a hand in protest. "I'm a prosecutor, remember?"

"I think you are a lawyer first," Schweitzer countered. "And how is it that we lawyers are able to convince people to believe some facts and disbelieve other facts when they are all, in fact, facts?"

Brunelle thought for a moment. "I'm not sure," he admitted. "Some facts are better than others?"

Schweitzer laughed. "Yes, that is it, but not in the way you think. It is not that some facts are better for us," he explained. "It is that some facts are better for them. For our audience. For my judges and for your juries."

Brunelle narrowed his eyes at his international colleague and nodded. He thought he understood. He was pretty sure he did what Schweitzer was suggesting, but not so consciously.

"People believe what they want to believe."

"Exactly!" Schweitzer slammed a thick hand onto the table. "That is the most powerful tool any lawyer has in his tool bag."

"Toolbox," Casey suggested. "We say 'toolbox'."

"Really?" Schweitzer asked. "What if it is a bag?"

"It's usually a box," Casey answered. "At least in metaphors. I mean, I have a bag with tools in it, but a toolbox is better. More storage space, better organization, that sort of thing."

Brunelle nodded. "Yeah, she's right. You should say toolbox."

"Okay," Schweitzer agreed. "Um, it is the most important tool in a lawyer's toolbox. The fact that people believe what they want to believe. Sometimes they do not even know that they want to believe it. It is simply that the fact confirms or corroborates other facts that they want to believe."

Schweitzer pointed to a waiter across the restaurant. "See that young man there? He is a waiter, yes? We can all agree on that. But is he a hard-working employee striving to earn money and make himself a better life, or is he an exploited member of the working class forced by circumstances to provide his labor to make the rich owner of this restaurant even richer?"

Brunelle thought about that for a moment. "Probably both."

Schweitzer slapped the table again and laughed. "Exactly what a lawyer would say." He pointed to Casey. "What say you, Detective?"

"I say," Casey answered, "it depends."

Schweitzer laughed again. "And that is exactly what a police detective would say. What does it depend on, hm? How much is he being paid? Does he like working here? Is he a student working part-time while earning a degree that will help him become the rich business owner? Or is this the end of his career goals? You want to know all that, and then you will conclude which fact is true. He is either exploited or he is not. You will discover the facts to make that determination."

Again to Brunelle. "But you, Lawyer. You accepted the limited facts as they were given to you, and you were prepared to argue either side. Your only hesitation was knowing which side to argue. If he was a crime victim, then he would be hard-working, yes? But if he was the criminal, perhaps not, hm? Perhaps he was ungrateful and greedy. It all depends on what you are asked to argue."

Brunelle shrugged. "A good lawyer can argue both sides," he defended.

"Yes," Schweitzer agreed, "but only a great lawyer can win both sides. And who decides who wins?"

"The jury," Brunelle knew. "Or in your cases, the judges."

Schweitzer smiled. "You would make a different argument to a jury of restaurant owners than you would to a jury of waiters, would you not?"

Brunelle nodded. "I definitely would."

"Would you try to convince the jury of waiters that our man is lazy and greedy?" Schweitzer asked. "Would you try to convince a jury of owners that he is being unfairly exploited?"

"No," Brunelle answered. "I would tell the waiters he was exploited and hard-working and explain why that made him guilty. I would tell the restaurant owners he was lazy and greedy and explain why that made him guilty."

"Then both of those juries would believe you," Schweitzer said, "because you told them what they wanted to believe."

"What they already believe," Brunelle understood.

Schweitzer grinned. "Even better."

He looked to Casey and Brunelle in turn. "Now, do you understand why you came to me and why you were wrong to do so?"

Casey shook her head. "No. I really don't"

But Brunelle nodded his. "I do."

CHAPTER 26

"People are who we think they are," Brunelle tried to explain later over coffee and sweets at a *Bäckerei* near their hotel. "At least they are to us."

Casey closed her eyes and shook her head. "No. They are who they are. If we think something different, that's our fault for not learning more about them."

"I can agree with that, to a point," Brunelle offered. "But only to a point. We don't have time to do all the research to determine who someone really is. We go on appearances. Sometimes that's all we have to go on. Especially if they're hiding something."

Casey thought for a moment. "Okay, I guess that's true. That's what I do for a living. So what?"

"So, I think that's why we can't figure this case out," Brunelle said. "We've let ourselves believe what we want to believe instead of what we should believe."

"Is there a plan in there somewhere?" Casey took a sip of her coffee. "Or is this just more lawyerly bloviating?"

"That's a big word for a cop," Brunelle laughed.

"Detective," Casey corrected. "And if the insult fits..."

"The plan is to start over," Brunelle said. "Try to look at this for what it is, not what we expected it to be."

"Start over?" Casey lamented. "We don't have time to start over. You heard what Schweitzer said. The case is barreling forward."

"I heard," Brunelle answered. "But I think I know how to slow it down. I need to be at that hearing tomorrow."

"But how?" Casey asked. "Sabine told you she had no more use for you."

"No, she left me an opening," Brunelle recalled. "I just need to be the prosecutor she wants me to be."

CHAPTER 27

"Hello, I'm back," Brunelle greeted the receptionist at the Berlin prosecutor's office. He still didn't speak German, but he knew she spoke enough English to understand the same request he'd made twice before. "I would like to see Sabine Ehrenwald, *bitte*."

That time, though, he was able to change his 'please' to a 'bitte'.

Nice touch, he congratulated himself.

The receptionist seemed less impressed with someone bothering to speak a single word of her language. She motioned for him to sit down in the usual waiting chairs and picked up the phone to call Sabine. Her sighs and eyerolls were a universal language even Brunelle could understand. But he was undaunted. He had 'A Plan'.

It took a few minutes, but finally Sabine Ehrenwald appeared in the lobby. "What do you want?"

Brunelle stood up. "And it's lovely to see you again as well, Sabine. Can we talk?"

"About what?"

Brunelle flashed what he hoped was a disarming smile.

"About what to argue when a murderer refuses to answer questions."

Sabine stood there for a moment, one arm still propping open the door back to her office. Her eyes narrowed, and she was just barely chewing the inside of her cheek.

"I thought you were too good to make such arguments," she said. "I thought you were an American hero, better than us Germans."

Brunelle shook his head. "No, I'm just a lawyer. A prosecutor, like you. I seek justice, just like you. I thought about what you said, and I realized I was something else. I was wrong."

That admission succeeded where the smile had failed. There was nothing more disarming than admitting you were wrong. Sabine's tense posture relaxed just a little. Just enough.

"Let me help," he asked her. "*Bitte.*"

It might be the only word he knew, but it was a good word to know.

"I still do not like you, American Hero," Sabine said absolutely unconvincingly, "but I will not turn down an offer to help me win a murder case." She pushed the door all the way open. "Come along."

Brunelle knew when to follow orders. He also knew when to follow a German prosecutor back to her office. He should have by then; he'd done it enough times. When they reached her office, Brunelle took his usual seat opposite Sabine's desk. She went ahead and sat down behind it. She was doing him a favor, not the other way around. No need to crowd him again.

"Let me start by apologizing," Brunelle began. His goal wasn't simply to have the conversation he'd managed to finagle out of her. It was to get the invitation at the end of that conversation. That meant offering some contrition to go with his assistance. "We Americans get brought up being told we're the greatest nation in the history of the Earth. Once we become adults, we get a better idea of some of the less perfect things we've done as a country, but that early indoctrination is hard to shake. Then, as a lawyer and especially a prosecutor, I spend my days dealing with all of the rights our constitution gives to people accused of crimes. And again, that early indoctrination makes me look down on any criminal system that's different from ours. But if I'm honest, there are definitely problems with the American criminal justice system."

Sabine raised a single eyebrow. "You don't say?"

"I do say," Brunelle responded. "But it took me a couple of days to realize that I wasn't willing to say it when you and I were having dinner. I should have been more openminded. I should have been more respectful of your system. I should have been more respectful of you."

Sabine's eyebrow lowered, but she was frowning. "So, you came here to apologize? I don't need your apology, Davey."

"I know that, Sabine," Brunelle answered. "But I wanted to let you know that after we talked, I thought about what you had to say. More importantly, I tried to think of an answer to your question. What's the best way to argue that a suspect's silence is evidence of their guilt? Once I got past my own mental barriers to that question, I started thinking about it, and I realized the answer to the question. Or at least the question to the answer."

Those eyebrows of Sabine's knitted together. "The question to the answer? I do not understand. Is that some sort of figure of speech?"

Brunelle smiled. "No, it's just me trying to be clever." He leaned forward. "You asked me, what was the best way to argue a suspect's silence meant guilt, and I realized there's another question that needs to be asked first."

"So, what is that question?" Sabine inquired, her eyebrows relaxing again.

"The question is," Brunelle pointed to her, "who am I making that argument to?"

"Whom," Sabine corrected. "To whom are you making that argument."

Brunelle paused. "Are you correcting my grammar? My English grammar?"

"Am I wrong?" Sabine asked.

"I, I'm not sure," Brunelle admitted.

"Obviously," Sabine sniffed. "I am not wrong. You make an argument to someone else, therefore the other person is the object of the verb and proper interrogatory is 'whom'."

Brunelle stared at her for several seconds. "I didn't really understand most of what you just said."

Sabine sighed. "I'm sorry I mentioned it. Well, no, I'm not sorry I mentioned it, but I am sorry we are still talking about it. Please, continue your presentation. You were saying? The question is, to whom are you making the argument, correct? That was your point?"

Brunelle leaned back again. "Um, I mean, yes. Kind of. I mean, it's an important point." He took a moment to get his train of thought back on the rails. "Who, or whom, are you making your argument to? Part of the reason we don't do it in the U.S. is because we would be making that argument to jurors, regular people not schooled in the law. There's a risk a prosecutor would just say, 'If you were innocent, you'd deny it, right?' and the jurors would just nod along and convict, even if there were good reasons for the suspect not to speak at that particular moment. But you, your system, that's different, right? You make your arguments to judges, not jurors. Your judges studied the law; they have law degrees; and they look down on everyone else from a place of education and knowledge. They've seen it all; they've studied it all; they know it all. Or at least," he raised a punctuating finger at her, "they think they do."

Sabine took a moment. "They do think that, yes."

"Exactly!" Brunelle enthused. He had her. "So, the challenge is not crafting an argument that will persuade them to believe what you say. The challenge is to craft an argument that will let them believe what they already think themselves."

Sabine took a few more moments. She steepled her fingers again and turned slightly in her chair as she contemplated Brunelle's words. Finally she turned back to him. "So, what is that argument?"

Brunelle smiled and pointed right at her. "I do not know!"

Sabine dropped her steepled hands into her lap.

"But I will find out," Brunelle hurried to continue. "I need to observe your judges in action. I need to come to court and observe them. See how they treat the litigants, the defendant, each other. I need to see how they see themselves, and then I will know what argument to make."

Sabine's nostrils flared. "You don't speak German."

"I know," Brunelle admitted. "But I won't need to. I've picked up some words—"

Like *bitte*. And sometimes *nicht*, if people weren't speaking too fast. Oh, and *danke*, although he kind of already knew that one.

"—but what I really need is an opportunity to see the judges reacting to your arguments, the defense attorney's arguments, and if possible, some sort of summary or listing of the expected evidence in the case." It was a statement, but his voice went up at the end almost as if it were a question. Which, really, it was. "Do you guys do anything like that?"

"You want to come to our hearing tomorrow," Sabine said. Again, a statement, but with a question weaved into it.

"You have a hearing tomorrow?" Brunelle hoped his previous interactions with Sabine would allow her to believe he was simply bumbling into the opportunity, rather than planning to exploit it. Let her believe what she already believed about him.

"I will not tolerate you and your girlfriend whispering back and forth," Sabine warned. "It is very distracting. I will not endure an entire hearing with poor translations floating in the air behind me."

"Oh, no, no, no," Brunelle assured. "She won't be there. She's a cop, not a lawyer. I don't need her for this. It would distract me too."

Sabine narrowed her eyes at him. After a moment, she sighed. "Nine o'clock. Same courtroom. Do not be late. And if you are late, sit in the back."

Brunelle gave her a sidelong glance and a charming, he hoped, smile. "So… if I'm on time, I can sit with you at the prosecutor table?"

Another sigh from his German counterpart. "If you are *early*, you may sit with me. If you are on time, then you are late, and you will sit in the back. Understood, Davey?"

"Understood, Sabine." Brunelle stood up and extended his hand to seal their deal.

A third sigh. But then she stood up and shook his hand. "Please don't make me regret this," she said. "Although I am certain that you will."

Brunelle tried again at that disarming smile. "Just this once, I will be happy to prove you wrong."

CHAPTER 28

That evening, Brunelle and Casey went over their plan. Which was good, because they were still making it up as they went along. Mostly, Casey was surprised Brunelle had pulled off getting the invitation to the court hearing, so they discussed what she would do while he was in court.

Start over at the beginning, they agreed. Which meant going back to the Balibai spa, and not for a massage. They had relied on Dieter's description of the event, rather than investigating it themselves. That is, rather than Casey investigating it herself. They had accepted their roles as witnesses. But if Brunelle was going to play prosecutor, Casey was going to play detective. While Brunelle was in court, trying to make sense of whatever evidence was being discussed in a language he didn't understand, Casey would be at the spa, examining a crime scene that had ceased being a crime scene some time ago.

A perfect plan.

Well, the beginnings of a plan anyway.

They parted at the hotel and Brunelle made his way to the

courthouse. He was in that same suit again and hoped it wasn't getting too gamey. If this kept up, they were going to have to find a dry cleaner near their hotel too.

The courthouse was exactly where they'd left it. Brunelle checked his watch as he reached the entrance. 8:53. He was right on time to be early so he wouldn't be late by arriving on time. All he had to do was find the courtroom and then saunter to the front of it to join Sabine Ehrenwald at the prosecutor's table.

"You're late," she growled as he completed his saunter.

He looked again at his watch. 8:56. "I'm early."

Sabine harrumphed. "Five minutes early is on time. Four minutes early is late."

Brunelle took a moment to ascertain whether perhaps she was joking. But her expression was as far from joking as he could imagine. It was her serious court face, which made her serious regular face look like a clown mask in comparison. She was obviously distracted, and probably anxious, about the imminent hearing, examining her notes and setting up her materials rather than keeping her gaze on him. Brunelle gambled she wouldn't want to waste time on an argument about the definition of early and late. Instead, he simply nodded, sat down at the prosecution table, and folded his hands.

Another harrumph from Sabine, but no argument. He was in.

The next to come in was Jürgen Schweitzer. Brunelle turned at the sound of the door opening and found himself mildly surprised to see Schweitzer actually walking into the courtroom. They had only ever seen Schweitzer seated and somehow Brunelle had pictured him entering the courtroom in a motorized wheelchair, as if he were too large to carry his own weight. But no, he was plenty capable of carrying himself into the courtroom. He was even bigger than Heiko and the floor actually shook as he approached the defense table. When he saw Brunelle, he offered a tip of his head and a, *"Guten Morgen, Herr* Brunelle."

That eyebrow of Sabine's raised again. "He knows you?" she asked Brunelle.

Brunelle tried to shrug it off. "I'm kind of a big deal."

Before Sabine could figure out what that even meant, let alone how to respond, the judge entered.

Small mercies, thought Brunelle.

What followed was a vaguely familiar ceremony involving the lawyers showing respect and deference to the judge, the defendant being brought in by armed corrections officers, and the judge placing himself figuratively and literally above everyone else by taking his seat atop the raised dais of the bench. But all in German.

Once everyone was seated, the hearing began.

And Brunelle had no idea what was going on. Obviously, he knew who was speaking at any given time, and he could tell the difference between an argument and a ruling, although only by whose mouth the words came from. But the details of the arguments were completely beyond him. He didn't even hear the word *'bitte'* although he wasn't surprised a room full of lawyers failed even once to say 'please.'

Brunelle knew it would be bad, but it was actually even worse than he'd expected. Maybe their plan wasn't that great after all.

Your plan, he could hear Casey say.

But he wasn't there for the words. He was there for the evidence. There was an advantage to not understanding what anyone was saying about the evidence. It allowed him to evaluate it all himself, without anyone telling him what it meant. Sabine would argue it was sufficient to allow the case to proceed. Schweitzer would argue it wasn't. The judge would declare whether it was. But Brunelle wouldn't be bothered by any of that. He could look at each individual item of evidence and make up his own mind.

If Sabine actually produced them, that is.

Brunelle had expected her to submit exhibits for the judge's review. Photographs and charts and physical exhibits, like bullets and guns—all properly secured of course. But after thirty minutes of nothing but speeches and counter-speeches, Brunelle started to wonder whether the 'evidence' to be reviewed by the judge was really only 'a description of the evidence' provided by the prosecutor, followed by a competing description offered up by the defense attorney. And judging by the pace of their unintelligible descriptions, Brunelle might be trapped there the entire morning, and all for nothing.

Then Brunelle got one more small mercy. Not that small, as it turned out. Sabine opened up one of the large binders on the table, revealing several dozen photos, each in its own plastic sleeve, each providing a detailed image of a piece of evidence the prosecution intended to introduce at the trial. And the photos weren't in German.

"Can I look at these?" he whispered to her. Schweitzer was up and talking at that moment.

"What?" Sabine seemed startled by Brunelle speaking at all. "No. No, of course not. Do not touch them."

But Brunelle was undaunted. "I can help," he insisted. "I could hand them to you, one by one, whenever you're ready for them."

"Eh..." Sabine seemed paralyzed by the unexpected offer from Brunelle. Her materials showed she was hyper-prepared, but sometimes over preparedness can lead to inflexibility. And being distracted by an American prosecutor can lead to missing the next thing the judge said.

"*Frau* Ehrenwald?" the judge called out. When Sabine's head snapped back to face the judge, the latter continued on in words Brunelle couldn't understand but a tone he'd heard more than once in his own professional life when he'd irritated a judge for one reason or another.

When Sabine addressed the judge again, no doubt to apologize, Brunelle went ahead and slid the first photo out of its plastic sleeve. He held it at the ready for when Sabine returned from apology back to advocacy.

It was a guess, but he guessed right. Sabine turned her attention to the binder only to find Brunelle had her first exhibit ready for her. She decided not to risk the judge's ire by whisper-arguing with Brunelle again, so instead she simply took the photograph and stepped forward to hand it to one of the judicial assistants seated directly below the judge. That person logged the photograph, then handed it up to the judge for inspection. At least that much was the same as what Brunelle was used to.

Even as Sabine walked back to their table, Brunelle extracted the second photograph from the binder. The first had been of the main entrance to Spa Balibai. The next was a framing shot of the ice plunge pool, Viktor Ferensz's head clearly visible at the top of the water. In the background were the narrow walkways between the sauna buildings, with a glimpse of the spa's wooden perimeter beyond.

Sabine snatched the photo from Brunelle's hand and renewed her address to the judge. Brunelle glanced again at the photo binder. There were a lot of photos. If Sabine was going to go through all of them right then, Brunelle might be spending the entire day in that courtroom, not just the morning. But it wouldn't be for nothing after all. He was getting to see the evidence firsthand, examining each photograph for several seconds before passing it to Sabine.

Another shot of the plunge pool, at a distance, from the perimeter fence, showing the long narrow walkway patrons took to enter the sauna buildings.

A closer shot of the plunge pool, Ferensz still bobbing in it. *Like a Halloween apple*, Brunelle thought, stifling a grin.

Ferensz's body out of the water, laid flat next to the plunge pool, pale and wet in the camera's flash.

A close-up of Ferensz's face, bloated, his hair stuck to his forehead.

Scenes from throughout Balibai. Every room, empty save the occasional foot or silhouette of another police officer.

The autopsy, Ferensz's body cleaned and dried and resting, sleeplike, on a metal examining table.

A close-up of the gunshot wounds. Two shots, center mass, the chest. He never had a chance.

Several more autopsy photos, showing the path of the bullets by peeling back, one by one, layers of yellow fat and red muscle, white bone and purple organs.

Then suddenly a scene change to Ginkel's arrest. Marched out of his apartment in handcuffs. Seated at the interrogation (or not) table. His mugshot.

The photos gave way to copies of paper exhibits. Handwritten witness statements. Bank records. Other papers Brunelle couldn't quite decipher because of the language barrier.

It took a long time, but eventually they reached the end of Sabine's binder. It contained most of the things Brunelle's cases usually had. Crime scene photos, autopsy photos, witness statements. The only thing he noticed missing was a photograph of the murder weapon. Never recovered apparently. Brunelle had prosecuted cases like that too. It was always nice to find the murder weapon in the suspect's apartment, but as often as not, they chucked it off a bridge or sold it to some random lowlife at a remarkably deep discount.

Brunelle took a moment to glance over at Ginkel. He was sitting closest to Brunelle, the mass that was Jürgen Schweitzer on the other side of him. Ginkel looked skinny and pale, even less healthy than the first court hearing. Hardly surprising after weeks in a jail cell. It made him look even more guilty, as if the shame of what he'd done was exacting a physical toll on him.

Young man, desperate for money, decides to murder his rich boss for revenge.

Looking at the pathetic man at the table next to him, Brunelle could believe it. He did believe it. And then he realized he wanted to believe it.

"Oh, crap," he whispered to himself as he raised a hand to his forehead.

"What is wrong now?" Sabine hissed at him under her breath.

"Nothing, nothing," he assured her. But recalling the photos he'd seen and suddenly aware of his personal desire to see Ginkel as the murderer everyone said he was, he whispered to himself, "Everything."

CHAPTER 29

Several hours later, Brunelle and Casey emerged from the subway station and Brunelle pointed to his left. "Baumstrasse is right over there."

Casey nodded. "You think she'll be home?"

Brunelle shrugged. "Only one way to tell."

In fact, there were several ways to tell if Mathias Ginkel's pregnant girlfriend was home, but there was only one they were going to try. That being said, it was probably the most accurate method. They were going to go to her apartment and pound on the door. Baumstrasse 1345. Brunelle hadn't made it all the way there last time. But this time he brought backup, in case they ran into another mob of teenage hooligans.

As luck would have it, they had an uneventful walk to Ginkel's apartment. His former apartment, anyway, before he moved to the Berlin jail. But Brunelle was hoping Ginkel's girlfriend was still there. He had some questions for her.

"Why are we talking to this girlfriend again?" Casey questioned as they strolled up Baumstrasse. "I mean, I understand generally, it couldn't hurt. But is there something specific we're looking for?"

There was, but Brunelle wasn't fully convinced he was right about what he saw in those evidence photographs. He was certain of what he saw, just not of what it meant. Ginkel's girlfriend could give him the background information he needed to confirm his suspicion. But he wasn't confident enough to share it with Casey just yet.

"Just a hunch," Brunelle answered.

"You're lying," Casey observed.

Brunelle shrugged. "We'll see."

They had reached 1345 and Casey looked at him. "That makes no sense."

Brunelle gave her a wink. "Doesn't it?" He pulled open the door to the apartment complex.

Casey took a moment, then followed him inside. "No, it doesn't. Not at all."

Brunelle checked the lobby directory, with its mismatched hand-scribbled names, and pressed the 'UP' elevator button. "Exactly."

Casey rolled her eyes, shook her head, and sighed, all at the same time. "Maybe you better let me do the talking."

"I would," Brunelle grinned as the elevator door opened, "but you don't know what we're here to ask."

Casey paused, then followed Brunelle into the elevator. "Checkmate."

* * *

The apartment still marked 'Ginkel' in the lobby was on the third floor. It wasn't the Ginkel apartment anymore though. It was the whatever-Ginkel's-girlfriend's-last-name-was apartment. It was also #32, which was helpful since there were no names on the doors, and they didn't know the girlfriend's name anyway. Brunelle rapped on the door, then stepped aside. In truth, Brunelle had no choice but to let Casey do the talking. Do the talking for him, that is.

It took a little too long, but just before Brunelle was about to knock again, the door unlocked and opened a few inches. A heavily made-up eye and that telltale blue hair was visible through the crack.

"*Ja?*" she asked cautiously. Brunelle didn't think they looked especially threatening, but it was a tough neighborhood. People were known to have been accosted just walking down the street.

Casey commenced with the introductions, and the explanations. Who they were, what they wanted, why she should open the door and let them in. It took a few exchanges, but Casey turned on the charm and soon enough, Ginkel's girlfriend invited them inside.

"Her name is Ina," Casey informed Brunelle.

He nodded. Progress already.

And more progress as they made their way inside the cramped, but remarkably well-furnished apartment. Brunelle looked around at the leather couches, polished wood tables, and enormous flatscreen TV mounted on the wall. Maybe Ginkel was doing a little better than they had thought. He should have looked at those bank records more carefully.

Everyone sat down on the leather couches and Casey turned to Brunelle. "So, what was it you wanted to talk to her about?"

"Hm?" It took a moment for Brunelle to pull himself back to task. "Oh, right. Um, ask her if Mathias ever owned a gun."

"Seriously?" Casey questioned. "That's the big reveal? Did he own a gun?"

Brunelle stared at Casey for a moment. "Yes, that's the big reveal. Did he ever own a gun? Did she ever see him with a gun? Did he ever talk about guns? Has she ever heard from anyone anywhere that Mathias ever shot a gun in his entire life?"

Casey raised an eyebrow. "All of that?"

"You get the drift." Brunelle urged her on with a roll of his wrist.

Casey shook her head but turned back to Ina. Brunelle wasn't sure if Casey was really asking all of the questions he'd suggested, but there were a lot of words. Certainly more than a single 'Did Mathias own a gun?'

Brunelle didn't understand the words Ina used to reply, but he definitely understood the shaking of her head as she answered. He also recognized the honesty in her face as she said it.

"She says, no," Casey confirmed. "Mathias never owned a gun, and she never saw him with one. Not many people play with guns, even in this neighborhood, and Mathias wasn't one of them."

"How long have they been together?" Brunelle followed up. "I mean, at least nine months, I'm guessing," he added with a nod toward Ina's swollen belly.

Casey smiled at the observation, then posed the question to Ina.

"Two years," Casey reported.

"Nice," Brunelle remarked. Then, "Tell her congratulations on the baby."

"Really?" Casey questioned.

"Yes, really," Brunelle defended. "We can't congratulate her?"

"We don't even know her," Casey replied. "And the

baby's father is about to go to prison for murder."

Brunelle clicked his tongue again. "We'll see."

Casey cocked her head at him, but before she could ask what he meant by that comment, he pushed himself out of the stiff leather of the still new couch.

"Ask her if we can see the nursery."

"What?" Casey asked. "Seriously?"

"Seriously," Brunelle confirmed. "Tell her congratulations, and ask her if we can see the nursery."

When Casey just sat there and stared at him, Brunelle sighed and added, "*Bitte.*"

Casey shrugged. "Yeah. Sure. What the hell."

Ina's replies included two words Brunelle actually knew: "*Danke*" and "*Ja*". She stood up and walked past Casey and Brunelle to a small, short hallway that led to the apartment's only bathroom, Ina's bedroom with its unmade bed visible through the doorway, and the small second bedroom that had been converted to a nursery.

A nursery right out of the Gucci Baby catalog. Or Rolls Royce Baby. Or something like that. Brunelle wasn't sure. He pulled a government salary. Good health benefits and a pension in exchange for middling wages and a vague satisfaction of making the world a better place.

Ina's nursery was stacked and stocked. Hardwood crib, overstuffed leather rocking chair, diapers and blankets and onesies filling the closet from floor to ceiling. She wasn't wanting for anything. So Brunelle finally asked.

Or Casey did, actually. But it was Brunelle's question.

"Ask her how she can afford all this," he directed.

Casey didn't argue that time. She put the question to Ina who answered it readily.

"She says she got money from Ginkel's boss," Casey reported. "He brought it to her because he felt bad about Mathias going to prison when she had a baby on the way."

"Spa Balibai?' Brunelle questioned.

He could understand Ina's response, especially with the shake of her head. *"Nein. Nicht Spa Balibai. Château Wunder."*

"Chateau Wunder?" Brunelle questioned. "Hans-Peter Oberflacher came here and gave her money?"

Casey asked the question. Ina nodded. *"Ja."*

"What did he look like?"

Casey listened to Ina's response, then turned to Brunelle. "It wasn't Oberflacher, Dave. Oberflacher is old and tall with gray hair. She said the man who brought her the money was younger, average height, with dark brown or maybe black hair."

"So, half the city." Brunelle frowned. "Well, we know it wasn't Heiko."

"Or Schweitzer," Casey agreed. "Anything else?"

Brunelle's frown deepened, but then it evaporated as he noticed the large wooden letters hanging on the wall above the crib. "Tell her 'Maria' is a beautiful name."

CHAPTER 30

Dinner that night was had at a little out of the way place that specialized in German food, almost a rarity in the city, it seemed. The crowd skewed older and less touristy than most of the Italian and Asian food joints. Most importantly, it was quiet, and their table was secluded in the back, so Brunelle and Casey felt free to assess their progress on the case aloud. Or rather, to reassess it.

"We fell into that trap Schweitzer was talking about," Brunelle said, raising his glass of red wine slightly. "We believed people were who we wanted to believe they were."

Casey nodded above her own glass of the wine. "He's right. Everyone does it. But we shouldn't have. *I* shouldn't have. A good detective follows the facts wherever they lead."

Brunelle shook his head. "You are a good detective. We didn't know we were going to get wrapped up in this case. By the time we did, it was already too late."

"And we didn't have access to all of the facts," Casey soothed herself a bit.

"We still don't," Brunelle pointed out. "All we have is

what we thought."

"And what we thought was wrong," Casey said. "Maybe."

Brunelle laughed. "Or maybe not. But let's go through them anyway. Who was the first person we encountered?"

Casey gave a dark chuckle. "Ferensz, I guess."

Brunelle nodded. "I guess so. What did we decide to believe about him?"

"Murder victim," Casey started. "Rich guy. Maybe deserved it."

"Probably deserved it," Brunelle suggested. "Because he was rich. So, dead rich jerk. Who next?"

Casey thought for a moment. "Dieter."

"Right," Brunelle nodded. "Nice guy. Friendly. Eager to be liked."

"Good at his job," Casey said. "Underappreciated by his boss."

"And by Sabine," Brunelle added. "So, nice guy, hard-working underappreciated detective."

Casey nodded at the description. "Speaking of Sabine, let's do her next. Cold."

"Mean," Brunelle added.

"Smart," Casey said.

"Sexy," Brunelle offered.

Casey laughed. "Really? You say that about another woman while we're on a date?"

"When do you want me to say it?" Brunelle parried with a joke. "I was just saying what you were thinking. Your word, not mine."

Casey thought for a moment. "That was very definitely your word." She shook her head at him. "So, smart and sexy prosecutor for Sabine, huh?"

"See? Your word," Brunelle pointed at her. He quickly moved on. "How about Schweitzer?"

"A very large man," Casey said diplomatically.

"A smart man too," Brunelle said. "At least I thought that after we talked to him the second time."

"Right, but these are first impressions," Casey reminded him. "What was your first impression?"

Brunelle frowned a bit as he considered. "Defense attorney."

"So…?" Casey encouraged.

"So… untrustworthy. Shifty. Duplicitous."

"Wow," Casey laughed. "You have some issues with defense attorneys."

"I have some experience with defense attorneys," Brunelle defended. "I didn't mean any of those things in a bad way. They have secrets to keep. It would be unethical for them not to be sneaky, shifty, and duplicitous."

"So, let's go with secretive defense attorney," Casey suggested. "Who's next?"

Brunelle took a sip of wine. "Oberflacher."

"From when we broke into his office?" Casey asked. "Or when we pretended to have tickets and made a scene?"

"Speaking of sneaky and duplicitous," Brunelle laughed. "Let's go with the scene at the ticket window. That's when we actually met him."

"Professional," Casey said. "Patient. Cultured."

Brunelle nodded. "Agreed. Respectable successful businessman."

"Ina," Casey suggested next.

"Pregnant," Brunelle responded immediately.

"She was really pregnant," Casey agreed, "and young."

"And loaded, apparently," Brunelle said. "Unless she spent it all on that nursery and the new furniture."

"She probably did," Casey opined. "So, young and pregnant girlfriend?"

Brunelle nodded. "Which brings us to Mathias Ginkel himself. What did we want to believe he was when we first learned about him?"

Casey thought for a few moments, a sip of wine fortifying her thoughts. "Guilty. We thought he was guilty."

"Exactly." Brunelle nodded. "I think we were wrong about everyone."

CHAPTER 31

During a career of helping people whose lives had been ruined by ruining other people's lives, Brunelle had learned to treat everyone with a certain level of respect. Everyone was human, no matter what they had done. But more importantly, he might have a use for everyone down the road, and there was no point in burning bridges just to feel righteous.

His time in Germany had been no different, so by the time he and Casey had finished their wine, and their schnitzel, and their desserts, they had a plan, but it relied on favors from some of the people they had already encountered. Luckily, they had treated pretty much everyone with that base level of respect. They had also lied to every one of them as well—bald-faced lies right to their faces—but they had done so respectfully.

They called on those select people, and they called in those favors, and then they waited for the plan to unfold. As a bonus, if all went as planned, Brunelle might get to see that second act after all. The plan was set to take place at Château Wunder.

Casey and Brunelle arrived first, but dressed down. They

tried to look like tourists who had no interest in paying for the actual show but were following their guidebook's advice to check out the amazing lobby. They were also trying to look at least a little different from those two idiots who demanded to see Oberflacher after coming to the theater on the wrong night.

The next to arrive was Ina Ginkel's-Girlfriend. They never did get her last name. She was dressed more or less like the other times Brunelle had seen her. It didn't matter. She wasn't trying to avoid Oberflacher. In fact, she was there specifically to see Oberflacher. Because Casey had lied to her again. But respectfully.

Brunelle and Casey took up a position in a far corner, from which they could see and hear but might, they hoped, not be noticed. Casey had to whisper the translations to Brunelle.

"She just asked one of the employees to see Oberflacher," Casey reported. "The employee asked who she was. She rubbed her belly and said, 'a friend.' Which is also the word for girlfriend in German," Casey explained with a chuckle. "The employee freaked out. He told her to wait there. He's going to get Oberflacher."

It took a few minutes, but eventually Oberflacher emerged from the back offices of the theater—the ones Brunelle and Casey had trespassed in. He marched quickly to Ina and made no effort not to look down on her, literally peering over his nose at the pregnant teenager.

"This should be good," Casey prefaced her translation. "She just asked him for more money. He's totally confused. He asked, 'Money?' then, 'More?' He says he has no idea what she's talking about."

"Which is true," Brunelle noted.

"Right," Casey agreed. "She's trying to explain that he

sent someone who gave her a bunch of money. Shit, it was over five thousand euros. But she says she needs more. She's worried about the baby. She wants to make sure the baby has everything she needs."

"Little Maria," Brunelle commented. "It is a nice name."

Casey shrugged. "It's fine. Whatever. Okay, Oberflacher is starting to get agitated. He just looked at his watch and told her he doesn't have time for games. He said he's in the middle of a very important meeting and only came out because the employee told him a young pregnant woman needed assistance. Ina is getting upset too. She said she's not going to take 'no' for an answer. She's not leaving without the money."

"Nice," Brunelle said. "She's persistent."

"Yeah, I told her to be," Casey said. "I told her he'd pretend not to know what she was talking about, but to stand her ground and refuse to leave."

"She listened to you," Brunelle said. "Smart."

"Learn the lesson, Davey," Casey quipped. "Always listen to me."

Brunelle grinned but didn't reply directly. "What are they saying now?"

"Oberflacher doesn't know what to do," Casey relayed. "He keeps telling her she has to leave, and she keeps saying 'not until I get my money'. She's getting louder, and he's getting flustered."

"Good." Brunelle nodded.

"Okay, there it is," Casey reported. "He said he's going to go get his head of security."

"Perfect," Brunelle said. He checked his watch. "Now, let's see if we got our timing right. Early is on time. I told her to arrive five minutes from now."

"And there she is," Casey laughed. Sabine Ehrenwald walked into the theater lobby, looking around for someone. For Brunelle.

"I'll go get her," Brunelle said, and he emerged from their hiding spot to fetch the German prosecutor.

Brunelle had lied to her too. He had used her obvious attraction to him, and her even more obvious discomfort with it, to convince her to meet him for an afternoon rendezvous in a cabaret theater lobby. It wasn't terribly respectful actually, but it was pleasant in the moment. And effective. "Sabine!" he called out, with a wave of his hand. "Over here."

"What is going on here, Davey?" she demanded with a scowl. She nodded toward Casey. "And what is she doing here?"

Brunelle didn't answer her questions. Instead he pointed at Ina shifting her weight uncomfortably on the other side of the lobby. "Shh. Just watch."

There wasn't much to watch for a minute or two until finally, Jürgen Schweitzer arrived. Casey had been the one who talked to him. Whether what she said had been a lie was yet to be determined. He hadn't needed any special convincing and didn't need any special instructions. He lumbered to the other corner of the lobby and turned to watch what happened next.

And what happened next was exactly what Brunelle and Casey had expected would happen. 'Hoped' might have been a better description, but they were fairly confident. It was exactly what they had deduced would happen.

Oberflacher returned to the lobby with his new head of security. Dieter Vorsburg.

He didn't see Brunelle or Casey, or Sabine or Schweitzer. But that was mostly because he did see Ina, and he froze in his tracks.

Ina pointed at Dieter and yelled something.

"She said, 'That's him'," Casey translated. "'That's the man who gave me the money.'"

"Nice," Brunelle commented.

"Now Oberflacher is confused," Casey went on. "He asked Dieter if he stole money from him. Dieter is assuring him he didn't. He's claiming he doesn't even know Ina. But she's insisting he was the one who brought her the money. She's saying he said it was from Oberflacher because Mathias worked there, but they had been paying him under the table, which is illegal."

"That sounds true," Brunelle said. "Except it's not."

"What is going on?" Sabine demanded again, although she whispered the demand, showing her willingness to go along and see what happened next.

"Just watch," Brunelle answered.

"And listen," Casey added. "Dieter is still saying he doesn't know her, but it's pretty obvious Oberflacher doesn't believe him. Oh, there! He just admitted he did take the money to her. But he insisted he didn't steal the money from the theater. It was the upfront bonus they paid him when he signed the contract to be the head of their new security team after Ferensz was murdered."

Sabine couldn't hold back anymore. She stepped out of their corner and shouted something at Dieter.

"She just asked Dieter, 'You're moonlighting?'" Casey informed Brunelle.

Dieter looked even more shocked than when he'd walked out and seen Ina. "Sabine?" he gasped.

"Ooh, she's pissed," Casey said. "She's asking if Leptheimer knows. Oh, and yes, how can he be the lead detective on a case when he benefitted financially from the victim's death?

It's a conflict of interest."

Brunelle and Casey finally stepped out of their hiding spot.

"That's not the real conflict of interest, Sabine," Brunelle announced, in English. "He didn't just benefit from Ferensz's death. He engineered it."

That evoked the gasps Brunelle had hoped for, although there was a brief delay as the native German speakers took a moment to understand his English words.

"That is ridiculous!" Dieter exclaimed. "Viktor Ferensz was murdered by Mathias Ginkel."

"That's what you wanted us to believe," Casey jumped in. "That's what we wanted to believe. We all want to believe the police do their job right. We all want to believe only guilty people are charged with crimes. So, when Mathias Ginkel was charged with the murder of Viktor Ferensz, we all wanted to believe it was true. You knew that. You counted on that."

"Lies!" Dieter shouted. "The video showed him hiding between the sauna buildings and shooting Ferensz."

"No, the video showed him disappearing between the sauna buildings just before the shots were fired," Brunelle retorted, "but they never showed Ginkel pulling the trigger. Because he didn't. He couldn't have."

Dieter frowned. An angry, teeth-bearing frown. "What do you mean he couldn't have?"

"Those shots were at least twenty feet away," Brunelle explained.

"Use meters," Casey suggested. "Seven meters away. They won't understand feet."

Brunelle's shoulders dropped. "Really? Right now?"

Casey shrugged. "I'm just saying. They don't know how

far twenty feet is. They know how far seven meters is. It's kind of important they understand this part. It's pretty much the key to the entire case."

"Fine." Brunelle looked up at the ceiling and sighed. "Seven meters. Those shots were at least seven meters away, but they hit Ferensz in the middle of the chest. Two shots, dead center."

"Exactly how they teach you to shoot when you become a police officer," Casey said.

"There's no way Ginkel made that shot," Brunelle continued. "But there's a very real way Ginkel went into one of the saunas to clean it out at the end of the day and when he did, you stepped out of a different sauna where you had been hiding and fired two perfect kill shots."

Brunelle pointed to Ina, whose expression showed she had no idea what anyone had said after the conversation switched to English. "Ina confirmed Mathias never owned a gun, but a police inspector not only would have a gun, he would know where to get a silencer, so Ginkel wouldn't hear the shot and go running up to help the victim. He'd just finish his shift and leave the spa, which is exactly what he did. That's why you never interrogated him. You didn't want to give him the chance to state his alibi officially."

Dieter was literally sweating, but wasn't ready to give in. "That is a nice fantasy you have crafted, but it makes no sense. Why would I murder Viktor Ferensz?"

"Actually," Casey stepped forward to field that question, "that was the other key to the case. The motive. No one could tell us why Mathias Ginkel would murder Viktor Ferensz. We spent all this time and energy trying to find his motive. But when we stopped assuming Ginkel was the guilty person and stopped looking for his motive, we instead looked for a motive and followed that to the guilty person."

"That doesn't explain why I would do it," Dieter insisted.

"You said it yourself," Brunelle answered. "You're bored as a cop. You'll never get promoted. You admired the idea of private police. And who can forget, rules are meant to be broken? Who better to head up a private security firm than a former police inspector? Well, *junior* inspector."

"And what better place to start that firm," Casey jumped in, "than as the in-house security for one of Berlin's fanciest and most popular cabaret theaters? You'd be sure to meet all of the city's rich and powerful, a perfect chance to sell your services at top dollar."

"Top euro," Brunelle interjected. "These people don't understand dollars."

Casey rolled her eyes at him, then forged ahead. "The only problem was, Ferensz wouldn't hire you. So, you got rid of him and used his very murder to convince his replacement of the need to hire you."

Dieter's eyes darted around the room. Oberflacher had taken several steps away from him as Brunelle and Casey laid out their theory. Schweitzer had come out of his own hiding corner and walked closer during the presentation. Dieter was facing a semicircle of hostile faces.

"Actually," Dieter said, finally, "I never asked Ferensz to hire me as private security. I knew Oberflacher would be scared enough to do it if his predecessor was murdered by one of his own employees. It had to be somebody close. Somebody in the building. Ginkel was as good as anyone, and when I found out he worked at the same spa Ferensz went to, I came up with the plan."

Dieter narrowed his eyes at his audience. "Don't judge me too harshly. I took care of his baby." He nodded toward Ina. "They'll be better off without him anyway, without having to depend on some loser who has to work under the table for tips."

"So, really, that's why you did it?" Casey cocked her head. "You murdered someone, and framed another person, just to start up a business?"

Dieter nodded. "Yes." Then he pulled a handgun out of the back of his waistband and pointed it at Casey. "Also, I wanted to see if I could get away with it."

He leveled the gun at the others. "Now, step back. All of you. I am leaving."

He started walking slowly backward toward the exit. He kept the gun trained on Brunelle and the others, arcing it slowly back and forth to menace everyone facing him. "Stay back." He warned. "Stay back or I'll shoot."

He turned to run out the door, but instead right into Heiko, who of course had followed Brunelle and Casey to the theater. Heiko grabbed Dieter's wrist and yanked him off the ground, the gun clattering safely to the floor.

"*Nein,*" Heiko told Dieter. "*Schieß nicht.*"

"Hey," Brunelle elbowed Casey in the ribs. "I understood that."

Casey smiled at him. "Good for you, Davey. Good for you."

EPILOGUE

"This has been quite the vacation," Casey remarked as they sat down in their VIP seats. "Nothing I expected and everything I didn't."

"In a good way?" Brunelle asked.

"Oh, definitely in a good way," Casey confirmed. "We caught a murderer, returned an innocent man to his family, made friends with a German defense attorney, and earned the grudging respect of a Berlin prosecutor. What more could we have asked for?"

"The eternal gratitude of the manager of Berlin's premiere cabaret theater," Brunelle answered. He gestured around them. "Complete with free front row tickets for that show I never got to see the end of."

"And that." Casey leaned over and kissed him on the cheek. She really did look great in that yellow dress.

"Shh," Brunelle hushed as the house lights dimmed and he pulled Casey closer. "Act Two is about to start."

END

THE DAVID BRUNELLE LEGAL THRILLERS
Presumption of Innocence
Tribal Court
By Reason of Insanity
A Prosecutor for the Defense
Substantial Risk
Corpus Delicti
Accomplice Liability
A Lack of Motive
Missing Witness
Diminished Capacity
Devil's Plea Bargain
Homicide in Berlin
Premeditated Intent
Alibi Defense
Defense of Others
Necessity

THE TALON WINTER LEGAL THRILLERS
Winter's Law
Winter's Chance
Winter's Reason
Winter's Justice
Winter's Duty
Winter's Passion

THE RAIN CITY LEGAL THRILLERS
Burden of Proof
Trial by Jury
The Survival Rule

ABOUT THE AUTHOR

Stephen Penner is an author, artist, and attorney from Seattle, Washington. He has written over 30 novels and specializes in courtroom thrillers known for their unexpected twists and candid portrayal of the justice system. He draws on his extensive experience as a criminal trial attorney to infuse his writing with realism and insight.

Stephen is the author of several top-rated legal thriller series. *The David Brunelle Legal Thrillers* feature Seattle homicide D.A. David Brunelle and a recurring cast of cops, defense attorneys, and forensic experts. *The Talon Winter Legal Thrillers* star tough-as-nails Tacoma criminal defense attorney Talon Winter. And *The Rain City Legal Thrillers* deliver the adventures of attorney Daniel Raine and his unlikely partner, real estate agent/private investigator Rebecca Sommers.

For more information, please visit *www.stephenpenner.com*.

Printed in Great Britain
by Amazon

39767797R00108